DATE DUE			
MAR 10			
MAR 17			
MAR 24			
		MAR 30	

TEACHERS' CHOICES

Cover design by Chris Van Allsburg

The Chinquapin Tree

The Chinquapin Tree

Jerry Kimble Holcomb

MARSHALL CAVENDISH   NEW YORK

Marshall Cavendish Corporation
99 White Plains Road
Tarrytown, New York 10591

Library of Congress Cataloging-in-Publication Data
Holcomb, Jerry Kimble.
The Chinquapin tree / by Jerry Kimble Holcomb.
p.   cm.
Summary: Fearing they will be sent from a loving foster home back
to their abusive mother, three children hide out in a secluded spot
on Oregon's coast, trying to find food and shelter
ISBN 0-7614-5028-9
[1. Survival—Fiction. 2. Brothers and sisters—Fiction.
3. Runaways—Fiction. 4. Oregon—Fiction.] I. Title.
PZ7.H69715Ch   1998   [Fic]—dc21   97-48554   CIP   AC

The text of this book is set in 12 point Galliard
Printed in the United States of America
1   3   5   6   4   2

Dedicated to my granddaughter
Cristin McDonald
and to
Vi Mosier
Peggyann Barrier
Marlene Lee

Chapter One

*J*essie Cloud ran hard down the beach, her long red ponytail bobbing from side to side. When she reached the trail, she paused beneath a clump of willows to catch her breath. Waves hissed along the shore behind her. A seagull squawked.

What if they came back today? Slivers of worry needled her mind. Jamming her feet into sandals, she dashed up the steep, sandy trail that came out at the edge of a wide field. She gazed toward the house, but Pop's greenhouses and clustered trees blocked her view.

She felt as if she were moving in slow motion as she crossed the field and pulled open the gate. In the driveway stood the white car.

Why are they here again? She tried to ignore the fluttery feeling in her stomach. It was the third time the Children's Services people had come to see Mom and Pop. Twice last week and now today.

Two women, *the same two*, came out onto the porch, walked carefully down the steps, and climbed into the car. Jessie watched as they backed the car out and drove off up the lane amid swirls of summer dust.

She closed the gate, then poked her head into a

bushy tunnel between the lilacs and the fence. Splashes of bright pink and yellow stood against the green leaves.

"Allie," she called softly.

The colors backed toward her from the depths of the tunnel until a head of black hair and two brown arms materialized.

Allie scrambled up, and her skinny arms clutched Jessie. "Are they gonna take us away?" she cried. "Will they send us back to Sherrill? Why don't they go away and leave us alone?"

"Don't whine, Allie," Jessie said, then wished she hadn't. Sometimes Allie acted so babyish for all that she was almost nine years old. "Maybe it's about Mom and Pop adopting us. They've talked about that, you know."

But Allie shook her head.

Jessie wrapped an arm around the younger girl's shoulder and felt her tremble. "Don't worry, Allie," she said gently, then asked, "where's Toady?"

Before Allie could answer, their younger brother dropped with a *thud!* from the maple tree beside the living room window.

She should have known he'd be up a tree somewhere. Where better to spy out what was going on?

Toady raced across the lawn and planted himself in front of Jessie.

"Mom's cryin'!" he exclaimed. "Those people did it!" His face screwed into an angry scowl and his blue eyes flashed.

Allie stiffened and her dark eyes opened so wide they seemed all whites.

Jessie pulled her sister closer. "Don't get all worked up," she said. "You'll bring on your asthma."

"They ain't comin' back on this place," Toady declared.

"Toady, calm down and tell us what they said."

Toady shrugged. "I dunno. I couldn't hear. They sat down at first, then one of them got up and handed Pop some papers, and then Mom put up her hands over her face, like this." He buried his face in his hands. "I know she was crying." Then they left, and Mom went to the kitchen."

Jessie looked up the lane, where thin dust still drifted above the field. She glanced around the yard, at the fish pond, the trees, the bright flowers blooming beyond the lawn, the big old house. We can't leave, she told herself. A knot tightened in her chest.

"Jessie, can they make us live with Sherrill again?" Allie asked.

Jessie looked away as she answered, "I doubt it." She dared not let them see the dread she felt. It would only frighten Allie. "Come on, let's talk to Mom."

Allie had let go of some of her fears in the two years they'd been here with Mom and Pop. But remembering Sherrill still upset her.

"Abused" was the word the social worker had used. Even when Allie was a baby, Sherrill never held her, just left her crying for hours in a rickety crib.

Sherrill yelled at all of them and made threats, and

sometimes hit them, but she seldom beat Jessie and Toady the way she did Allie. Sometimes Jessie took the blame for things—dumb things nobody could help—to spare her younger sister. Like once when Allie spilled ice cream on the floor, and Sherrill screamed and hollered and threatened to "rub your nose in that mess." "I bumped her," Jessie had said.

"She wasn't watching out," Sherrill shouted, and then added what she always said. "She's just like *him*." Then she spat out a curse Jessie didn't like to hear.

She meant Allie's father, although Jessie wasn't sure how she knew that. She didn't even know Allie's father. She remembered the man they called Wynn who had lived with them for a while before Toady was born. Toady, with curly, blond hair and bright blue eyes, looked like a small version of Wynn. The man worked in the strawberry harvest and sometimes brought her and Allie a basket of berries, and Jessie had hoped he'd stay. But when the crops were done he'd left.

Other men had lived with them for a few weeks at a time, but no one who could have been Allie's father. No one with skin the color of milk chocolate.

She sighed, refusing to push her thoughts further, to ask the secret question: *What about my father?* Everything about their family was such a puzzle.

I should have stayed here today, she thought now as they crossed the lawn. Mom and Pop's wasn't like the other foster places where they'd lived. From the first day it had seemed like their real home. Still, sometimes Jessie liked to be alone. Ever since she'd discovered the huge chinquapin tree on the bluff, she'd claimed it as her special place. A place where she could read and dream and just be Jessie Cloud.

Mom understood. "A twelve year old needs some space," she said. Of course Mom didn't know about the tree. Or how she'd found it. Nobody did.

Spicy smells floating from the kitchen met them even before they reached the steps. Toady raced ahead and yanked open the screen door; its hinges creaked. Mom turned from the sink where she was washing pans beneath a torrent of water. Her eyes looked red and swollen.

The children filed into the sunny yellow kitchen, then stood silent. Jessie couldn't think what to say.

"Dinner'll be ready in a bit," Mom said. "Go on in and watch TV with Pop till I call."

"I'll help," Jessie told her. Allie and Toady stood soberly beside her until Jessie motioned them to the other room.

"Mom? You okay?" Jessie asked when they were alone.

Mom looked at her for a long moment. Her sturdy figure seemed to droop and her dark eyes looked troubled. "Of course. I'm fine, Jessica." She took off her glasses and wiped her brown forehead with the tail of her apron.

"Those people put me way behind with dinner though. Good thing I had the chicken ready for the oven." Mom heaved a sigh. "Jessie, would you set the table?"

Jessie counted out five napkins and place mats.

"Set the good dishes—the ones with the big roses that Allie likes."

"Why? Are we having company?" Jessie had already taken down the plain white plates.

"No. But sometimes it's nice just to use things you like. Don't you think?"

"I guess." Jessie put the white dishes back and went to the other cupboard. Her finger traced the raised roses on the top plate. "Mom, what did those people want?"

Mom lifted the lid from a pan on the stove and steam spiraled upward.

For a moment Jessie thought she wasn't going to answer.

"We'll talk about it later, hon," she said in a husky voice.

Jessie frowned as she set five rose plates on the round wooden table.

Chapter Two

*J*essie laid the last fork in place. Now. She should ask now: *Do they want to take us away?* It was her best chance. While the kids watched TV and before Mom called dinner. Her mouth filled with saliva and she swallowed hard, trying to get her nerve up. Maybe she didn't want to know.

"Jessie, get a tub of margarine from the pantry. Do you mind?"

Too late. By the time she got back, Pop and the kids would be gathering around the table.

She crossed through the utility room, opened the door, and almost stumbled over Allie, who sat on the steps chewing the tail of her blouse.

"Allie! What are you doing out here?"

Allie peered up at her. "Did you ask her?"

"Not yet."

"But you will? You will, won't you?" Allie jumped up and clung to Jessie, almost crowding her off the narrow board walkway. The pantry, an old milk-cooling room left over from the days when this place had been a dairy, stood a few feet from the house. The shed where Pop kept tools crowded the other side of the walk and made the passageway dim and cool.

"Probably."

"You have to!" Allie grabbed Jessie's sleeve.

"Don't get frantic, Allie. You'll make yourself sick."

She tried not to sound annoyed, but she heard the sharpness of her own voice.

She opened the heavy door silently. The windowless room with its thick walls felt like a cool, dim cave where outside sounds were muffled. Jessie touched the light switch, illuminating shelves that lined two walls from floor to ceiling and held every sort of canned vegetable and fruit, along with plastic canisters of cereals, noodles, spaghetti, and rice. Beside them stood a refrigerator and a chest freezer. Braided garlic and bunches of drying herbs hung from the ceiling and filled the room with the scent of sage and mint. Camping gear hung from the walls, and Mom's big canner kettles filled a nearby table.

Allie stood against the door, holding it open. She looks like one of those pictures of starving kids you see in magazines, Jessie thought. Only Allie certainly wasn't starving here. That look was because of her asthma—and because of Sherrill.

Sherrill would strike out at any of them, flailing them with her fists or with whatever was handy. When Toady was little she spanked his bare buttocks hard whenever he had accidents, all the time screaming at him, telling him he was bad. If Jessie said something she didn't like, Sherrill cursed and struck her, sometimes knocking her down. They'd all learned to keep an uneasy silence when Sherrill was home, especially if she'd been drinking. Still, it was Allie she beat as though she couldn't stop.

Jessie stood remembering the time Toady had

found a little snake. Of course he'd wanted to keep it, and Jessie didn't really mind snakes, but Allie's eyes had grown wide, and she'd cringed in the farthest corner of the yard. Sherrill had brought her back and forced her close to the wriggling thing. Jessie could still hear Allie's piercing screams.

"You gotta learn not to be scared of things," Sherrill had yelled. With each scream she'd brought the snake closer to Allie's face. In one motion Jessie had grabbed and flung the thing hard over the high fence and instantly felt the sharp sting of a slap across her face. But it was Allie who got the beating. Sherrill had whipped off the black leather belt she always wore with her jeans and smacked Allie's legs again and again. Jessie had been helpless, knowing that if she interfered Allie would get it worse. She remembered the hateful look on Sherrill's face.

We won't go back no matter what! she told herself. Just thinking of living with Sherrill—they never called her "Mother"—made her insides churn.

"Jessie?" Allie's voice brought her back to the present. "You s'posed to get something?"

"Yes," Jessie said, still engrossed in her thoughts. Absent-mindedly she took a yellow carton from the refrigerator. She told herself it'd been that beating— when Allie's teacher reported the belt marks, purplish streaks across her legs—that got them away from Sherrill. Again.

After a few months in yet another foster home, they'd come here.

"Jessie, Mom's calling you," Allie insisted.

Jessie closed the pantry door and followed her sister into the kitchen. The yeasty smell of hot bread filled the room. Mashed potatoes steamed on the table, and Mom was just placing a platter of crispy chicken next to it.

"What on earth took you so long out there?" she asked. "I thought maybe you went to town for it." Mom grinned and Jessie knew she was teasing. "Come on, Toady and Pop," she called. "It's gettin' cold."

Jessie took her place between Allie and Mom at the round table. Pop sat opposite, with Toady beside him. They bowed their heads and held hands while Pop said the blessing.

"How come the special dishes, Mom?" Pop asked. Jessie saw Mom give him a glance. He grinned and placed two drumsticks on Toady's plate. "Sure nothing like Mom's baked chicken, is there?" He passed the platter on to Mom.

"I think tomorrow we'll let the nursery take care of itself. Toady and I are going fishing." Pop said.

"All right!" exclaimed Toady, his mouth full of chicken.

"I heard today the perch are running. August, that's the best month to catch them."

"I'm gonna catch a hundred!" Toady cried, swinging his arms as though landing a fish.

"Careful there," Mom said, laughing as she steadied his milk glass.

"Sorry," Toady said. Turning back to Pop, he begged, "Can I fish from a rock?"

"I reckon you're big enough now not to fall in the surf. After all, a boy that's going on six . . . "

"Seven!" Toady corrected, holding up as many fingers. "I'll be seven next month."

Pop shook his head. "There I go again, getting all mixed up." But he was grinning and they all knew he was joking, trying to keep things light.

He hitched a strap on his bib overalls as he reached for the plate of chicken. "Come on, kids," he said, "eat up."

For some moments only the sound of dishes clinking broke the silence. Jessie's throat tightened so she could hardly swallow. Allie pushed her food around on her plate and hardly took a bite. Mom didn't even urge her to eat, as she usually did, but told her, "I made that strawberry dessert you like."

When they'd finished eating, Mom glanced over at Pop, and it was as if some sort of signal passed between them. As she pushed back her chair and stood up, she said, "Jessie, let the dishes go for a bit. All of you come into the living room. We have something to tell you."

Chapter Three

"But why do we have to leave?" Toady demanded from his seat on Pop's lap. "I ain't goin'. I'm stayin' here with you and Mom."

Pop had fixed popcorn for all of them before they settled in the living room. There, Mom explained about the women from Children's Services.

"They said someone from Portland, from Multnomah County, would be down in a week or so," Mom had explained. "They want you back in Portland, where you'll be close to your mother." Mom's voice sounded husky, and she held tight to Pop's hand while she talked.

"Why?" Jessie cried. She hadn't meant to sound so explosive.

Mom sighed and spread both hands in a helpless gesture. "I don't know, Jessie. Maybe it's because we want to adopt you. Or maybe there's some other reason."

Half-hidden by Mom's chair, Allie sat cross-legged on the floor, looking scared. She put one kernel of popcorn into her mouth.

"Those women said your mother was home again and wanted to see you," Mom added in a quiet voice.

"Huh!" The single word erupted from Allie as she hid her face. Was she crying?

"We are going to adopt you," Pop asserted. "We

might run into a snag or two, but we'll work it out."
He looked from Jessie to Mom, then added, "I called
a lawyer in town this afternoon. He'll get an order to
stop them from taking you away, at least temporarily.
That'll give us some time."

Relief left Jessie feeling weak.

"Some people have this nonsense about skin color.
Don't like mixing. But I figure the mixing's already
been done," Pop went on.

Jessie knew he was right. More than once in Portland they'd been all set for a certain foster home. Then
when the people saw Allie's brown skin they made
some excuse. But Jessie always figured she knew the
real reason. She'd worried all the way on the trip down
here that they'd just have to go back to Portland and
start over.

But as soon as she saw Mom's dark skin and Pop's
freckled white, she knew things here were different.

"My goodness, what beautiful children," Mom had
said as she'd wrapped her arms around the three of
them. "A blond, a brunette, and a redhead. How
lucky can we get?" She had smiled at Mrs. Gates, the
social worker. "We're going to do just fine."

"What if that lawyer can't stop them?" Jessie asked
now. She thought of other times they'd been moved
from one foster home to another. The other times
hadn't mattered. They were just places to get away
from Sherrill. Here was different. This was home.
Mom and Pop were like their real family. We never
had a family before, she thought.

Even school was different here in Mills Beach. Teachers treated them like regular kids, not fosters. And last year, in sixth grade, Jessie had even made a friend, something she'd never done before because it hurt too much when they had to move.

It was such a puzzle. Why would Children's Services want to move them? Always before, there'd been a reason, like people had too many kids, or moved away, or somebody got sick.

"Now look here," Pop said, as he sat up in the big, brown leather chair. "We're going to do everything in our power to keep you kids here. Forever." He said the words with such fervor that even Allie raised her head. She wasn't crying, but her face looked pinched.

"That's exactly right," Mom declared. "We just wanted you to know what's happening. Now, don't worry about a thing. But when those people come back, you kids just make yourselves scarce. Go to the beach or over to the woods there until they leave. Pop and I will do all the talking. Understand?"

All three nodded.

"Now, it's been a long day, so off to bed."

"Can I take my popcorn?" Allie begged.

"Go ahead," Mom said. "I'll be along later."

Allie and Toady ran up the stairs.

"Jessie," Mom said, placing a hand on her shoulder. Jessie glanced around the room, at the comfortable chairs, the worn carpet, the soft photos of flowers on the walls. Home.

"Don't let those people get to you," Mom went on. Her dark eyes held a kind of pleading. "It's all going to work out."

"I know," Jessie said, feeling awkward.

"And Jessie, I know you like to go off by yourself, but for now maybe you should stay close."

She knew Mom meant to watch out for Allie and Toady. That meant no more going to her tree.

"Except maybe Saturdays. Those people don't work on weekends," Mom added, heaving a sigh.

Jessie nodded and started up the stairs.

She heard the commotion before she reached the landing. And when she opened the door to her and Allie's room, the floor was strewn with popcorn. Toady stood, half hidden by a screen, grinning, a handful ready to throw. When he saw Jessie he crammed it into his mouth, looking sheepish.

"What's going on?" Jessie demanded. "You guys pick up every kernel!"

Making a face at her, Toady chanted, "Bossy, bossy, we don't have to."

Jessie glared. She hated it when he said that. "Okay, then leave it. See what Mom says when she comes up." She shut the door and crossed the hall to the bathroom.

How can they act so scatterbrained when our lives are falling apart? She splashed water over her face and jerked the tie from her hair, letting it fall loose around her shoulders. Was she bossy? Maybe. It came from looking out for them since they were babies, she guessed.

When she went back the popcorn was cleaned up and both children were in their pajamas, sitting soberly on Allie's bed.

Jessie closed the door, and Allie came and stood looking up at her. Her black hair frizzed around her head, nearly hiding her face. Jessie bent forward and teased, "Are you in there?"

"Don't!" Allie said, as she wiggled closer. "Jessie, why don't those people want us to live with Mom and Pop?"

Jessie took a deep breath. She guessed she'd rather have them throwing popcorn. "I don't know." She took Allie's brown hand in her own. "But you aren't to worry. You heard Pop. The lawyer'll know what to do."

"But can they make us live with *her*?" Allie demanded.

"We'll have to wait and see," Jessie said.

"I don't want to go back there." She sounded close to tears.

"We won't have to, Allie." Jessie wished she felt as certain as she sounded.

To her relief, Mom and Pop came in then.

"What has eyes and can't talk?" Pop asked, grinning.

"It's can't *see*," Toady corrected.

"Oh, did I get it wrong again? But you didn't answer."

Allie and Toady shouted in unison, "Potato!"

"What has ears and can't see?" Pop joked.

"It's *hear* and it's corn," Toady said, rolling off Allie's bed and grabbing Pop's legs.

Mom sat beside Jessie, laughing at the frolicking. She reached out and smoothed Jessie's hair with her hand. "It's getting so long," she said, "and the sun's put golden glints in it."

Jessie smiled. Most redheads hated their hair. But for Jessie it was like a mark that made her who she was. Besides, she'd decided a long time ago that her father must have had red hair. Sherrill's was plain brown.

Pop lifted Toady and carried him into his room. Allie lay down and pulled the sheet over her. Mom gave Jessie a hug and kissed Allie good night. "See you all in the morning," she said.

Chapter Four

$\mathcal{T}$he next few days were edgy. Jessie jumped up to look every time she heard a car out on the county road. Mom forgot to take meat out for dinner one day, and on another couldn't remember whether she'd fed the chickens. When anyone asked her a question she looked blank, as though the words weren't getting through.

Allie whined or burst into tears over nothing at all. Pop and Toady went fishing, and each time Toady burst into the kitchen grinning and holding up a string of small brown fish. "I caught ten of them," he exclaimed one day.

On Friday Pop drove to town to see the lawyer, but when he came back all he'd say was that the lawyer would "see what could be done." Jessie winced at the defeat.

Saturday morning she got up early and hurried downstairs. Carrying her bowl of cereal into the yard, she sat on the edge of the fish pond to eat. A spot of sunlight dazzled through tall fir trees. The air felt fresh and cool, but the hazy blue of the sky told her today would be another August scorcher.

She finished eating and hurried back upstairs. She already knew the tides by heart, but she flipped the pages of the tattered tide book and checked again.

She smiled, remembering how confusing the tides had seemed when she first came here. But Pop had taken them to the beach and pointed out the thin line of debris far up the sand where the waves had reached that morning. "That's where high tide reached," he told them. "Now, about six hours later," he said, "it's nearly low." They walked close to the water. "If you'd been standing here at high tide you'd have been in deep water. Keep that in mind."

He'd explained that tides are measured above or below a fixed point called zero. "When you have a minus tide, that means it's below that fixed point. That means it's extra low."

Jessie had studied the tide book each day until checking the tide became as easy as looking up a phone number.

"Low at 9:07 this morning," she said aloud. "A minus tide at that."

"That's really low," Toady said from the hall floor where he sat pulling on his shoes.

"Time to get up, Allie." Jessie called, as she smoothed the spread over her bed. Jessie picked up a stray sock and put it in his hamper.

"Allie, come on. I want to get done."

"Why? So you can run away and leave us?" Allie cried, sitting up. "I saw you looking at the tide book!" She flung back the covers and threw herself out of bed.

Jessie stood with her back to Allie for several moments. "Not fair!" she wanted to shout.

Allie marched from the room, leaving her bed unmade and her clothes strewn about on the floor.

I should just leave her mess, Jessie thought. But she picked things up and straightened the untidy bed.

Half an hour later she hurried toward the beach, an apple and a book in a denim bag slung over her shoulder.

A slight breeze blew, and the sun baked her bare shoulders as she ran to the edge of the surf and slipped off her sneakers, then shivered at the rush of cold water sloshing over her feet and ankles.

Above the beach a tangle of thorny brush discouraged intruders, and the state park was over a mile in the other direction. So usually she had this lonely stretch to herself. Sometimes she sang songs or played pretend without worrying about prying eyes and felt as free as the gulls that soared overhead. But today each bird screeched, *Not free! Not free!*

The low rumble of the ocean calmed her as she walked along, scuffing her feet in the hot sand. The fishy-seaweedy smell told her the tide was already far out. Waves came in partway, then backed off, as though something sucked at them from underneath.

Half an hour later the sand gave way to a wide expanse of tide pools, and beyond that a hulking black cliff that extended far into the ocean blocked her way. Although she'd been curious about what lay on the other side, Jessie had found it impossible to climb over the sheer rock wall or to find a way around it. Until that day last February.

Storms had lashed the coast for days. Gale-force

winds and driving rain sent waves churning and boiling and breaking as though the sea had gone mad. Hunks of driftwood were tossed in the surf like twigs. The storm's fury made tree branches writhe and twist, and crashing waves rattled windows.

When it was over the sun came out, warm and bright, as if to triumph over the winter storm.

As soon as the ocean calmed down, Jessie had hurried to the beach to see what the surf had brought in. When she reached the cliff, she'd stopped short. Part of it had broken loose. An enormous heap of boulders, red earth, and crushed succulents spilled over the beach.

Jessie had picked her way over and around boulders, some higher than her head, until she came close to what remained of the cliff. That's when she'd found it: an opening in the rock several feet above the beach. A cave, she thought at first.

Holding her breath, she'd climbed up and crept inside. The ocean thundered and echoed around her. Ahead, she spotted a speck of light. She took cautious steps forward, goosebumps on her arms. What if the ocean washed in from the other side and caught her? The light speck grew larger until she came out onto a narrow ledge of rock along the cliff's edge. Waves churned and slapped only a few feet below. Beyond, a wide, sandy cove beckoned.

Now, just as she had done that first time, she clambered through the opening and edged her way across the ledge, steadying herself against sheer rock.

"Whew!" she said as she dropped to the sand. "Toady and Allie could never do that. They'd be too scared."

She ran through the mist that rose from the wet sand and climbed the hot dune to a bluff above.

At the top she stopped to marvel at the tree. Her tree, standing off to itself like a huge coppery-green mound, secretive, its branches brushing the ground. She'd never known a tree could grow so big.

Some distance above her the Bjorset house clung to the hillside, looking like a mansion with bare windows staring down. But she needn't worry because Inge Bjorset, who lived there alone, was gone for the summer. The newspaper said she was traveling on the continent.

"Continent!" Mom had scoffed. "Like this wasn't a continent. Why don't they just say, 'Gaddin' around in Europe'?" Mom didn't take much to what she called high-falutin' talk.

Jessie ran to the tree and ducked beneath its branches to its cool shade and half-darkness. Like a huge room carpeted with leaves and moss. The tree's enormous limbs swooped low like smooth, gray sofas. It must have been here even before white men came, maybe forever.

Hidden among its leaves were spiny burrs. She plucked one and gingerly parted the top, pricking her fingers on the sharp needles as she fished out a single nut. She cracked it with a rock and popped the kernel into her mouth. Too bad they're so little, she thought.

Once, she'd carried a cluster home and showed them to Pop. "Chinquapin," he told her. "That's what the Indians called it." He'd spelled it for her, then added, "But around here we say 'chinkapin.'" When she complained about the stickers, he'd said a most peculiar thing: "The reward hard earned is better enjoyed."

Now, she swung herself onto a low branch and climbed almost to the top, where she settled into a seat formed by two crossed limbs. Taking out her book, she opened it to the bookmark.

But her thoughts would not stay on the story.

What would the lawyer be able to do? she wondered. Could the Children's Services people make them go back to Sherrill? Worry jangled at her mind until she felt consumed by it.

What if they did come today? What if they *did* work on Saturdays? Her heart began to pound with fear. What if they took Allie and Toady away and she never found them? It was a fear they'd always held, each time they had to change foster homes—being separated and losing each other.

She slammed her book shut, dropped quickly from limb to limb, then ran, skidding down the hot dune through flying sand. When she'd crossed the narrow ledge, she splashed through the tide pools, never mind that her sneakers got soaked. By now her head roared. Why had she left the house at all?

She raced, stopping only to catch her breath or when a stitch in her side doubled her over. Finally she stumbled across the field to the house and collapsed, breathless, on the back step, her shoes clotted with wet sand.

Toady and Allie, playing on the tire swing Pop had hung from an old maple tree, didn't even notice her.

Chapter Five

*N*early two weeks passed before they heard from Children's Services again.

It was late one afternoon, the fifteenth of August, an unbearably hot day, with no breeze coming off the ocean. Mom fixed a pitcher of lemonade, and they all sat under one of the big maple trees out front. Jessie peeked at her watch every little bit, knowing that those people went home at five o'clock. Though no one ever mentioned it, only after five o'clock had passed would they laugh and chatter freely.

It was four-fifty when the white car came down the drive—a different car. On the license plate, in small letters below "Oregon," Jessie read "Multnomah Co.," and her breath caught. Allie pushed herself up from the green lawn chair and stood as if frozen, her dark face the color of ashes as she let out a moan. Jessie sat still as the car came to a stop. A tall man unfolded himself from behind the wheel and walked toward them. Pop got up and went to meet him.

"Mr. Harmon?" the man asked.

Pop said, "That's right."

"I'm Lyman Richards." He handed Pop a card.

"Have a chair," Pop said.

The man glanced around, looking at each of them—at Toady soberly clinging to Pop's hand and

Allie looking scared. Jessie refused to look away, but stared back, though she clenched her teeth together so hard her mouth ached. She wanted to yell, "Go away and leave us alone!"

His glance moved on to Mom, and the faintest hint of a smile touched his lips as he took a tall glass from her hand. "Thank you," he said, then placed the glass on the wooden picnic table. He dropped onto a bench, sitting stiff and straight.

Like a store mannequin, Jessie thought. Even his sleek black hair looked painted on. There wasn't a wrinkle in his gray suit, and his shoes were as shiny as Mom's dining table. Maybe he wasn't real. What if she reached out and touched his arm and it was plastic—or whatever mannequins were made of? What if it fell off and lay on the ground?

"Mr. Harmon." The man took papers from his briefcase and stared at them. Was he reading his lines from them? "I am here to inform you that we will be returning the Cloud children to Portland."

"Oh!" Mom sounded like she'd had the wind knocked out of her. Allie clutched Jessie's arm so hard her fingernails bit into flesh.

He handed the papers to Pop. "I believe you'll find these in order. We will pick the children up tomorrow at 2:30. I would appreciate your having their things packed."

"You can't do that," Mom said, getting up. "We—"

Pop put his hand on her shoulder. "Sir, we have talked to an attorney and—"

"Mr. Harmon, it is a matter of jurisdiction. These children are wards of the court in Multnomah County." He stood up before going on. "They should not have been placed out of county to begin with. It is our responsibility to decide what is in their best interests."

"But they are happy here," Mom said.

"Yes, I'm sure they are. Your care has been commendable. Nevertheless—"

Pop interrupted. "It's because we asked to adopt them, isn't it?"

The man cleared his throat. "I wouldn't know about that." He handed Pop a sheet of paper, then stepped back as though ready to leave.

Jessie jumped up, feeling lightheaded.

"Where will we live?" she asked.

The man looked at her. "You are Jessica, I believe?"

She nodded.

"I'm sorry, that has not been determined," the man said, his face expressionless. He looked straight into her eyes without blinking.

"Not back to Sherrill?" Jessie said, her voice too shrill.

"I presume you mean your mother?" When Jessie didn't answer, he went on. "We try, whenever possible, to reunite families. Your mother wants you returned to her. But that decision will be made later."

"You can't take us back there!" Jessie heard herself shouting. "She hates us. She's said so lots of times. Especially when she's drinking and doing drugs and stuff. Besides, she beats Allie." She felt Mom's hand on her arm.

The mannequin stood motionless.

"Mrs. Gates said . . . " Jessie went on.

"Mrs. Gates is no longer with our agency. She made a mistake placing you in another county. Now—" He paused and looked around at them. "—it is our job to rectify that."

He turned and walked stiffly toward the car, then turned back and added, "Your mother has completed two treatment programs, Jessica. I believe you will find her decidedly changed. She wants to provide a home for you."

"She does not!" Jessie felt her face go hot, and her head filled with ringing. "And she's not our mother! We're just accidents that happened to her!"

"Jessie! Don't be disrespectful" Mom's sharp voice stopped her. Never had Mom spoken to her in that tone.

Jessie whirled and ran toward the house. Why did tears always flood out of her eyes whenever she got mad? Why couldn't she stand up to him and say what she wanted to say? And why did adults always use that word just when you were making your point? *Disrespectful!* Had she done the wrong thing? Had she caused more trouble for them all? But she couldn't keep the words back. She couldn't!

Chapter Six

*J*essie headed straight for her room, taking the steps two at a time. She had to get away. She had to think. It wasn't until she opened the door to go in that she realized Allie was right behind her.

"What's going to happen, Jessie?"

"I don't know. You heard the same thing I did."

"But they're gonna take us away," Allie moaned, clutching Jessie's arm. "We can't just go away and leave Mom and Pop and *never* see them again."

"Be quiet!"

Allie shrank back and glared. "Don't yell."

"I'm sorry. But, Allie, I need to think."

Allie flopped across the bed and sobbed.

"Look," Jessie said. But when Jessie touched her shoulder, Allie jerked away.

Turning toward the window, Jessie watched Mom and Pop. Toady still held Pop's hand. The man stood facing them. Abruptly he climbed into the car, backed around, and drove away. Pop placed an arm around Mom as they walked back toward the house.

Jessie felt quivery. Two-thirty tomorrow. She looked at her watch. Five-twenty now. Not even a whole day before they'd be gone. But where? *That has not been determined.* The man's words clattered in her mind.

"I'm not going to be dragged away by that man-nequin!" she said suddenly.

Allie raised her head. "What?" she asked in a puzzled voice.

Mom's footsteps sounded on the stairs, and moments later she came into the room. Toady followed, his blue eyes looking scared.

"Girls," Mom said. Her voice trembled. "Don't worry. Even if they take you tomorrow, we'll go to court and get you back. Now remember that." She stood, wringing her hands. "Pop's downstairs now getting hold of that lawyer."

Jessie felt as if she were moving in a dream, as if this weren't really happening. She followed Mom downstairs and stood at the door to the living room.

Pop's voice thundered, "What do you mean we can't do anything?" He grunted into the phone a couple of times, then hung up.

"We can't even file here," he told Mom. "And he doesn't want to handle it." Pop pointed to the phone. "Says we should go to Portland and get an attorney up there." He looked helpless as he added, "He says we have no rights." A spot of red stood out on each of his pale cheeks.

"What?" Mom's voice came out shrill. "Why didn't he tell you that in the first place?"

"There's nothing we can do. We can't even . . ."

Jessie heard no more. Her knees felt weak and her face grew hot. The blood pounded in her temples as she stumbled into the living room.

"Why can't you do anything?" Her voice roared in her own ears and she couldn't tell if she was yelling or whispering. "If we were your *real* kids you wouldn't let somebody snatch us away!" Her eyelids burned and the door rushed toward her. No, she was rushing toward the door. Outside.

"Jessie!"

She heard Mom call, but she ran. Through the gate and up the lane. She ran until her side pained and her throat felt glued shut. She didn't stop until she was deep in the woods beyond the county road. Dropping to the cool moss, she pressed her sweaty face in it. She felt shriveled up, and everything seemed hopeless, hopeless.

Jessie lost track of time as she lay, trying to blot out everything. When she finally raised her head, the woods had grown dim and the blue was gone from the sky above the treetops. Thoughts kept worming their way into her mind. At last she said it aloud: "We never belonged anyplace before. And we don't belong now. Kids like us don't have a place. Maybe we'll never have a place because we're different."

After a long while her breathing came easier, and she sat up and peered through the shadowy woods.

"We have to make our own place." She spoke the words to the silence about her.

An idea was forming in her head. She'd taken care of all of them lots of times before, times when Sherrill didn't come home for days. Usually there wasn't any food in the house, but they'd managed.

They'd found things. Half-empty boxes of crackers, chunks of moldy cheese in the refrigerator. They'd hauled out bags of beer cans and bottles and used the refunds to buy bread and peanut butter.

"I took care of us before, and I can do it again," she said.

An urgent need to be with Allie and Toady made her leap to her feet and turn back the way she'd come. Stumbling over clods and roots in the darkness, Jessie found her way back to the field. Beyond were the road and the lane to the house. At least it was lighter out here.

Hazy gray clouds had gathered in the west. Not the kind that meant rain, but the sort that always followed hot days here close to the ocean. Beneath the haze was a sort of peach-colored glow. It held as she followed the lane and came into the yard. Fir trees beyond the house were ink blots against the sky.

Jessie stood a long time looking at the house. Somebody else's house!

"Another place where we once lived," she said aloud. "Like all the others." Tomorrow they'd be gone. *But it wasn't like all the others.*

Some places they'd been had felt like home. She'd settled in. But always there was that edge of knowing in her mind. Knowing that nothing was forever, so that when they had to leave she could shrug and tell herself, "I knew it wouldn't last."

Here had been different right from the start. They'd belonged. Taking care of them wasn't just a job to Mom and Pop. For one thing, their clothes came from real stores, not thrift shops, and right from the start they'd had chores.

Pop had partitioned off the big room so they each had their own space.

"Put anything you like on the walls," Mom had said, "cause you don't ever have to take it down."

"So we felt safe!" Jessie's words rang out in the silence.

Like believing the stories in her books were real! The ache in the back of her throat threatened to choke her, and the blood pounded in her head.

Forget that! she told herself. Forget it all. It's over, over, over.

The glow beneath the clouds had faded to a dull, watery yellow, and the trees melted together like a black wall.

An idea began to form in her mind as she walked around the outside of the house, and she shuddered, thinking of the danger. Still . . .

Something brushed against her legs and startled her.

"Fielder!" she cried, recognizing the big bear of a dog from the next farm. "You're always slipping around so quiet." She rubbed behind his ears, and the dog stayed beside her. She should send him home, but it was comforting to have another creature here with her.

Jessie stopped in front of the living room window. Toady sat on Pop's lap, both of them looking at a book, while Allie worked on the tangles in her embroidery thread as she huddled beside Mom's chair. Allie could untangle even the hardest knots, patiently worrying at them until they came out.

Another time she, Jessie, would have been curled in a chair reading. *Just as if nothing had changed!*

She wanted to march in there and scream, "Don't you know it's over? It's not real. Stop pretending!"

Instead she flung herself away from the window and headed for the kitchen door, the dog following silently.

"Go home, Fielder!" she scolded him. "Be glad you have a home!"

It's the only chance we have, she told herself. Forget the danger. She'd go up the back stairs and get things ready.

But as she opened the screen door, the creaking sounded as loud as an alarm. The kitchen sprang to light, and Mom and the others stood framed in the doorway.

"Jessie!" Mom said, wrapping her arms around her. "Where have you been? I'll bet you're starved." Mom held her close, and for a moment Jessie wanted to rest against her shoulder and feel safe again.

Then she stiffened, drew back, and forced a smile. "I'm not hungry." She looked away. "I don't feel good." That was true. "I just want to go to bed."

"We can stay up till eleven," Toady offered. "Mom said."

"Jessie," Mom pleaded. "Come sit with us awhile."

"No." The word came out abrupt, sharp.

Mom sighed. "All right, dear. We'll talk in the morning." Her arm dropped from Jessie's shoulder.

It was like coming to the end of a favorite book. Half of her wanted it back. No, no, she told herself.

"Now look here, Jessie." Pop spoke for the first time. "They may take you away tomorrow—I don't know if we can stop that—but we'll have you back soon, and don't you forget it."

She glanced up, and his eyes met her own.

"This is your home. Forever. No matter what happens."

Chapter Seven

$\mathcal{J}$essie climbed the stairs, forcing herself not to look back, and went into her room, so familiar but now changed. As though she'd already left it.

Stop that! she told herself. Hadn't Pop said he'd have them back?

She pulled from a hook the windbreaker she wore to the beach and dug in the front zippered pocket for her tide book. Sitting on the edge of her bed, she studied it. Two in the morning! That's when the tide was lowest. A minus tide, -1.1. The water would be far below the ledge, and they should be able to cross until three o'clock. Maybe later.

Her mind began to click off ideas. If she took them to her tree . . . They could carry enough food to last for a few days. And each one could carry a sleeping bag. Except she'd have to carry stuff across the ledge. At least that would give Pop some time. She smiled thinking of the mannequin's face when he came tomorrow and found them gone.

Jessie flew around their rooms, grabbing an extra pair of jeans for each one, a sweatshirt, underwear, and socks. They'd have to make do with one pair of shoes each, and they'd wear their jackets. She stuffed the clothing into her swimming bag and shoved it under her bed.

Next the sleeping bags. She slipped down the back stairs, finding her way across the kitchen to the utility room without turning on a light. She opened the door that led to the outside pantry. Pitch blackness between the buildings forced her to feel her way along, to take care not to trip over the uneven boards.

"Flashlights," Jessie whispered. "And batteries."

Those were stored with the camping gear. Light was one luxury Pop allowed when they went camping high in the wilderness that he called the "upback." "None of those softy camping parks for us," he always said. "That's not real camping."

She waited until the pantry door closed behind her before touching the switch that flooded the room with a yellow glow.

She found their sleeping bags, tightly rolled and stuffed into waterproof bags for easy carrying, two flashlights, and an extra pack of batteries. Thin plastic tarps to spread under the sleeping bags. And Pop always made them carry several large trash bags. "Handy for lots of things," he told them. She shoved a handful in with her sleeping bag and added a bar of soap.

Food. What should she take? She set out a large jar of peanut butter, two boxes of crackers, and a bunch of little cans of meat from the shelf. Lightweight cans that Pop kept for camping. How would they ever carry so much stuff? They'd need a can opener and plastic spoons and forks, too. She added a paring knife and several nested margarine tubs.

Fruit. The kids needed fruit. Apples and bananas.

What was she forgetting? Once they were gone they couldn't come back. Why couldn't she think ?

She peeked into the freezer. Frozen hot dogs wouldn't spoil if they ate them right away.

She'd wait and stuff everything into her own back-bag, the pink and lavender one Mom and Pop had given her last spring for her twelfth birthday. She debated over a package of marshmallows and finally put in several more little cans instead.

A glance at her watch startled her. Ten forty-five already. *Hurry!* She turned out the light, then found her way back through the dark kitchen and up the back stairs to her room.

Moments after she crawled into bed, she heard voices and knew Mom and Pop were bringing the kids up. She closed her eyes and pretended sleep, scrunching her face into the covers so Mom couldn't tell if her eyes blinked.

But Toady came running in, and immediately the smell of warm, buttered popcorn teased her senses.

"Hey, Jessie, we brought you some popcorn," he cried, shoving a big bowl under her nose.

Her stomach convulsed with hunger.

"Come on, Jessie."

Jessie sat up and grabbed the bowl and stuffed a handful into her mouth, then smiled sheepishly at Mom.

"Can I bring you something else?" Mom asked.

Jessie flushed. "No," she said reluctantly. She felt

ravenous but dared not waste time.

"I know you're worried," Mom said, stroking Jessie's hair.

Jessie wanted to apologize for her rudeness earlier, but if she did she'd fall apart. I have to keep strong, she thought. For all of us.

"Don't you worry," Pop put in. "In a few days we'll get this all straightened out."

Jessie grinned at him, feeling guilty for her secrecy.

After the kids were tucked into their beds and Mom and Pop had gone down the hall to their own room, Jessie lay staring at the ceiling, tracing with her eyes the shadowy lines cast by a night light near the door.

"I must not fall asleep," she whispered. A glance at the red numbers on the digital clock startled her. Eleven-ten already! She'd wake Toady and Allie at midnight.

How long would it take to walk more than a mile to the rocks? An hour?

Half an hour to get started, an hour to the rocks, that would be one-thirty. Still plenty of time to cross. Anxiety gnawed at her. What if she'd read the tide table wrong? What if she'd counted wrong? She went over the time again in her mind.

She pictured the things she'd gathered to take. Sleeping bags, clothes, food. They'd wear their jackets. They'd need them nights, especially if the fog rolled in. Had she forgotten anything?

She rolled onto her side and stared through the window at the dark patch of sky. How could she get

Toady to go with them without his making a fuss? Allie wouldn't be a problem. But Toady would ask a million questions. She propped herself on her elbow to keep awake.

Toady's cap from the Mills Beach Garden Center lay on the floor beside the night light. He must have dropped it earlier. Usually all of his hats hung neatly above his bed. A Donald Duck one with a big bill, another he'd gotten at the Oregon Aquarium, and his favorite, Adventure Man from a show on local TV. Suddenly she knew exactly how to coax him to go with her.

Allie stirred and coughed. *Allie's asthma medicine!* Jessie flung back the covers and tiptoed downstairs to the kitchen. Mustn't turn on a light. Mom kept Allie's medicine in a cupboard above the sink. Jessie ran her hand along the shelf until she found the bottle of pills and Allie's cough syrup.

She hurried back up the stairs and tucked the two bottles into her zippered jacket pocket. Shivering, she crawled back into bed.

"Jessie, where you been?" Allie's voice startled her.

"Shhhh," she said. The red numbers on the clock said eleven-forty-five. Time enough to tell Allie.

"Come over here," she whispered.

At once the tiny figure flew under the covers and snuggled in, her bare feet like ice on Jessie's legs.

"Have you been out of bed?" Jessie asked.

"Uh-huh. I was looking for you."

Jessie held back the annoyance she felt. "Allie, I'm

going to tell you something, but don't make a sound. Just listen. It's important. Understand?"

"Sure," Allie said.

"Now, look. If we stay here, that man'll come back tomorrow and take us away."

"I know," Allie said soberly.

"So, I have a plan for us to run away."

"Run away?" Allie whispered.

"Just for a few days until Pop can do something to stop them."

"Oh." After a moment she asked, "Where'll we go?"

"Never mind that now. But I'll need your help."

"Sure. " She snuggled closer, shivering. "What do you want me to do?"

"First off, don't make any noise. Then, when I wake Toady up, you two go down the front stairs to the living room. That's quieter because of the carpets."

"Are we going to tell Mom and Pop?"

"No, we can't do that. But this is what they'd want us to do. Go where we'll be safe from those people. See?"

"Uh-huh."

"I have our clothes in a bag under my bed. Take that with you. Don't talk at all. If Toady does, just say 'shhh.' "

"I wish Mom and Pop were going, too."

"Well, they can't just now. See, they have to be here tomorrow when that man comes. If they took us somewhere, that'd be kidnapping. But if we go ourselves, that's different."

"Can I take my Barbie dolls?"

Jessie started to say no, but stopped herself. Maybe the kids needed something to keep them busy. But they were already taking so much stuff.

"Sure, but only a few, okay?"

"And my sewing?"

"Sure."

Eleven-fifty.

"We might as well get up now," Jessie said. She threw back the covers, and Allie rolled out of bed. "Here, get dressed and stuff your pajamas in the bag." She handed Allie a pair of jeans and a sweatshirt. "And these socks and your tennis shoes. And put on this jacket. And hurry."

Jessie went to Toady's room and gathered up a few of his cars and stuffed them in with their clothing. "Put your dolls and sewing in here, too," she told Allie. She held her new paperback book for a moment, then decided it wouldn't take much room.

"Okay, quiet now. I'm going to wake up Toady."

Jessie stood beside his bed for a moment. He slept soundly as always. She shook him gently, but he only mumbled. "Toady," she said, softly.

"Uh-mmmmm" was the only response. He flung an arm out and rolled to the other side of the bed.

"Toady, wake up."

Gradually he sat up, rubbing his eyes.

"Whas th' matter," he grumbled, still half asleep.

"Toady, Allie and I are going outside. It's sort of an adventure. Do you want to go with us?"

"Whafor?" He stretched and yawned.

Jessie repeated her explanation. "Do you want to go? You can be our leader and wear your Adventure Man hat."

He sat up and looked at her. "Where're we going?"

"You'll see."

He stretched his neck and leaned way back. "How come you want me to be the leader?"

"You're almost seven, old enough to be a good leader."

He slid from beneath the covers to the floor in one motion, and began putting on his shoes.

"You'll have to get dressed. Come into our room. Your clothes are in there." He followed her, still yawning.

"Jessie—"

"Shhhh. Here, put on your special hat."

He pulled it down on his head and stood up.

"Put on your jacket."

"Jessie, is everyone all right?" Mom called.

"Fine, Mom." Her heart almost stopped.

She was the only one not dressed. She motioned for the others to be quiet and slipped into the hall, closing the bedroom door behind her. Mom stood at the door to her bedroom.

"I'm fine, Mom," she said, "just going to the bathroom."

She started to cross the hall to the bath. If only Mom'd go back to bed.

"The others sleeping?"

"They've been asleep for a long time." It wasn't a lie, exactly.

"Well, then. Good night again." She disappeared into her own room.

Jessie went into the bathroom, waited a few moments, then flushed the toilet. She hurried back to the room. They would have to wait now to be sure Mom was asleep again. She might not go back to sleep, she was so upset.

"Why can't we tell Mom and Pop about our adventure?" Toady whispered.

"It's a surprise," Jessie whispered back. Allie sat leaning against her, while Toady lay on his stomach dancing two of Allie's stuffed animals along the floor.

"Toady, shhhh," Jessie said.

He squinted up at her. "How come you're whispering?"

The clock said twelve-fifty when she finally decided to risk it. "Go down the stairs as softly as you can." Now they'd really have to hurry.

Toady straightened his Adventure Man hat, grinned at Jessie, and tiptoed into the hall.

Chapter Eight

*N*o one spoke until they reached the pantry. Inside, with the door closed, Jessie switched on the light.

"Everybody will have to carry something," she said, handing each child a sleeping bag.

"Are we gonna camp?" Toady sounded unbelieving.

"Sure," Jessie told him. "It's part of the adventure."

She stuffed each child's clothing and toys into backpacks.

"Put on the packs," she told them. She helped Allie while Toady shucked into his. Jessie strapped the sleeping bags above their packs. Pop had done a neater job when they went backpacking.

"I can't carry that much," Allie complained.

She did look overloaded. "Look, give it here," Jessie said, "I'll put our stuff in this bigger pack, and you'll just have your sleeping bag." Reluctantly she laid aside her lavender bag and stuffed clothes and food into Pop's larger brown backpack.

"I can carry mine," Toady boasted, strutting around the center of the room.

"We'll take it slow," Jessie said as she shrugged the pack on and fitted her sleeping bag on top. *But not too slow.* She glanced at her watch. One-forty. Almost low tide right now. "Okay, let's go."

The heavy pack pinched her shoulders and hung

too far down her back. For a moment she considered leaving the large jar of peanut butter behind. Better keep it, she decided.

"You said I could be the leader," Toady said, pulling his Adventure Man hat down.

"Sure, Toady. Just head for the beach." She handed him a small flashlight and kept the larger one herself.

"The beach? Are we gonna fish?" Without waiting for an answer he called "Onward!" in a loud whisper, mimicking his favorite hero as he marched across the field.

Allie grinned and trudged after him, her sleeping bag sagging to the right.

They stayed in shadows cast by the long green-houses, then went single file down the steep bank. When they reached the sand, Jessie said, "Go south first, Toady, all the way to the water,"

"Are we going to the caves?" he asked, sounding excited.

"No. We'll fool the enemy," she said in a deep Adventure Man voice. "Don't want to leave any clues."

It would take longer to walk south first, but once they reached the wet sand they could head back in the other direction, and the high tide would hide their footprints before morning.

"Onward!" Bounding over a driftwood log, Toady shouted, "Follow Adventure Man!" He ran, his light dancing along the beach.

As soon as they reached the tide line, they headed

north, walking in the hard, wet sand. "Remember, Adventure Man and his followers are on a secret mission," Jessie said.

"Onward!" Toady shouted, racing ahead.

Alarmed by the sound of gravel being pulled seaward, Jessie said aloud, "Low tide. Already." She shined her light over the smooth surface. Good, no wind swells to toss waves high up on the ledge. We'll make it across. If we hurry.

Jessie shifted her load constantly. The straps cut her shoulders. Was there anything they could do without? No, they needed everything. Maybe more.

They walked in silence, only the sound of the ocean and their feet on the sand.

Toady kept slowing down, and Jessie moved forward trying to hurry them on. Finally, he complained, "You're walkin' too fast. I'm goin' home."

"I'll slow down," Jessie said. But not too much, she added to herself.

After several minutes, Allie asked with a groan, "How much farther, Jessie? I'm tired."

"And my legs hurt!" Toady stormed. "You're still walkin' too fast." He stopped and stood glaring. They were less than halfway to the cliff.

"We'll stop at that big chunk of driftwood and rest," Jessie said, shining her light ahead. Allie's sleeping bag was about to drop.

"Here, Allie, let me take that." Awkwardly, she slung it over one shoulder, but it rolled off. Without stopping, she tied the two bags together, letting them dangle in front of her. She glanced back and saw that Toady had started walking again.

When they reached the large, flat piece of driftwood, Toady and Allie sprawled across it. Jessie dropped the load from her numb shoulders.

Toady took off his hat and demanded, "How come we have to do this? I want to go back."

"We can't, Toady," Allie said.

"How come? How come that man wants to take us someplace?"

So, Toady had already guessed why they were leaving.

"He wants us to go back to Sherrill," Allie said.

Toady crossed his arms over his chest. "Well, I ain't goin'! They can't make us."

In the dim light Jessie's eyes met Allie's.

"We don't want to live with her, either. Not ever!" Allie said. "But if we go back they'll make us."

"Look, we'll rest a bit and be good as new," Jessie said.

Toady rested his head on his sleeping bag and said no more.

Jessie sat listening to the low rumble of the ocean, staring into the empty blackness behind them.

Far back and high up a single light gleamed. We forgot to turn off the light in our room! Jessie longed to race back, crawl into bed, and let everything go on just as it had for the past two years. Pretend the mannequin had never come. Pretend they still had a home.

A fire began deep inside and seethed through her. Just a joke they play on kids like us, she thought. For the second time that day she reminded herself that they weren't like ordinary kids, that they'd never belong anyplace. Not for long anyway.

Chapter Nine

Jessie turned the light to see her watch. Past two-thirty! They had to get beyond the rocks before the tide came back in. "Come on, load up," she said, hefting her own pack onto her back.

The others groaned but gradually started moving once more.

"I can't carry this," Toady said, letting his sleeping bag drop in the sand.

"You have to," Jessie said. "I can't carry everything."

"I want to go home." He sounded close to tears.

"Toady, pick up your bag and come on!"

"No!" He planted his legs in the sand and scowled at her.

Allie moved close to him. "Come on, Toady," she said softly. "You want me to carry your bag?"

Toady seemed to sag. "No, I'll carry it," he said with resignation.

"Look, we'll leave both your sleeping bags here," Jessie said. She dropped Allie's to the sand. "Now run on ahead. I'll come back for them."

The waves crashed against one another as though fighting, and the kelpy smell told her it was well past low tide.

When they reached the wide stretch of tide pools, she slung off her load and raced back.

Would they be too late? No! She mustn't even think that! Her throat burned by the time she returned. She played the light over the dark rocks, many already wet with the inrushing waves.

She made two trips to get everything over the huge boulders. Hurrying, she waded right through the shallow pools.

"Look, Jessie, we can't go any farther," Toady cried as he came to the solid rock wall.

"I know a secret passage," she said mysteriously.

She'd have to take them across one at a time. But first she had to find a place to leave their stuff.

She shined the light around, hunting for a flat place where she could stash their things, but all the rocks were pointed and were surrounded by water. At last she located a trough where two rocks leaned together. Maybe she could wedge everything in there. It was awfully close to the incoming waves, but it was the only spot.

"Allie, come hold the light," she called.

Allie shivered, standing knee-deep in a tide pool, but held the light while Jessie fitted the bags into the narrow space one at a time. She weighted the ties on the sleeping bags with a large rock.

"They'll be safe for a bit," she said. "Come on, let's hurry."

Toady had already climbed the few feet up the rock cliff and was searching for a way through.

"Stay right there," Jessie told him.

"I'm cold," he said, shivering.

"Where're you going?" Allie sounded frantic when Jessie left her.

"Wait here. I'll be right back."

"Jessie! Don't leave me!" Allie grabbed Jessie's sleeve.

"Stay right there," Jessie commanded, prying Allie's fingers loose. There wasn't time to argue.

"Sidle around this rock," she told Toady, pointing the light toward the opening. "There's a ledge on the other side, like a shelf. Swing yourself through." When Toady didn't move she added, "Here, let me go first."

A wave crashed on the other side, echoing ominously.

"No, Jessie, I'm scared."

"Put your foot right where I'm shining the light."

She could feel the darkness behind her over the water, like something waiting to suck her in. I'm as scared as they are, she realized.

"Give me your hand and I'll help you." The rocks were wet now. Always before when she'd crossed, the sun had dried them. Were they slippery? She didn't dare look down.

Toady stretched his arms toward her.

"Easy now, this isn't very wide. Step over and pull yourself around."

"I can't feel no ledge. I'm gonna fall in the water."

"No you won't. See, I'm standing on it. Just a bit more, Toady, easy now." A wave hit the rock, its spray soaking her, and Toady pulled back with a cry.

"It's okay, you're almost there," she said.

Little by little he edged through the narrow opening, until he stood on the shelf of rock.

"Steady yourself by keeping your hands flat on the cliff, see? And walk sideways, like this." She began to move toward the cove.

Toady shuffled his feet a few inches at a time. "Oow," he shouted when another wave spewed both of them. She wanted to tell him to hurry, but she dared not.

"Only a few more feet, Toady," she said, keeping her voice calm and even. At last they were across and Toady jumped down onto the hard sand.

"Wow!" he exclaimed, shining his light around. "How'd you know about this?"

"Just wait right here while I go back for Allie," she told him. "Don't go anywhere, you hear?"

"Sure, Jessie."

Allie peered through the opening when Jessie got back. She climbed through and clutched Jessie's arm, her frail body rigid.

"I'm scared," she said. She grabbed Jessie as a wave splashed them. "I can't stand it!" she screamed. "You're trying to kill us! I'm going back."

Jessie hung tight to her arm and pulled her along the ledge. "Toady?"

"I'm here," he said, turning the light so Allie could see to climb down.

"I was scared to death," Allie said when she reached the sand.

In her hasty return, Jessie almost lost her balance. Careful, she told herself.

When she reached the rock where they'd left their things, she caught her breath. The water had reached dangerously close. She wedged the flashlight into a chink in the cliff, found footing on a nearby rock, and managed to grab the two packs. But she needed about six hands to get back to the ledge. She used up precious moments finding a lower step where she could climb up with her load.

She threaded herself through the hole, then inched the backpacks through the opening. She flung Toady's lighter pack over her shoulders, but no way could she carry the heavier one and keep her balance. At last she rested it on the ledge, then pulled it along with one hand. Step, shuffle, slide the pack. Step, shuffle, slide. Too slow, but she dared not rush. Every wave splashed her now. She kept her right foot and the hand that guided the pack glued to the wall of rock, moving only inches at a time. Once, when a wave hit, she wobbled and felt light-headed with fear but managed to steady herself. In the blackness how would she know when she'd reached the end?

"Hey, Jessie," Toady called, and suddenly light, like a beacon, lit up the stepping-down rocks, already surrounded by puddles.

"Here," she called to Toady and Allie, tossing the packs to the sand. "Take them way up the beach."

She rushed back for the sleeping bags. But as she

came through the tunnel, she cried out in dismay. A wave had caught the topmost bag and carried it several yards into the surf. A feeling of helplessness made her stand staring as each wave buoyed up the plastic covering, taking it farther away with each surge.

"Now!" she screamed to herself when waves lifted a second bag and bounced it from side to side.

The rock she'd braced herself on earlier was underwater. She leaned toward the rocks. Her fingers stretched and touched the ties, but the bags swished in the waves, tearing them out of her hands.

Jessie pulled back and, using the flashlight, peered down at the rock where she'd stood earlier. How deep was the water? Did she dare chance stepping down? Maybe with one foot? Then she could reach and get a grip. The surf swirled around the rock.

Another wave raised one bag, bouncing it precariously. Jessie gasped, then felt weak as the bag settled back against the trough.

Her heart pounded as she stretched again. *Wait until a wave goes back out. Now!* She teetered precariously, balanced between the cliff and the trough until her fingers held both cords. She yanked as she leaped backward and pulled the bags across the dark abyss.

She stood trembling, crumpled against the rock wall. A wave churned around the rock where she had stood, and another crashed over the top of the trough.

Hurry, she ordered herself. But how would she carry them? Not on her back. That could tip her into the ocean. There was no place to leave one. Besides, the water might be too high on the ledge to make another trip.

Finally, hands shaking, she wrapped the cords across her shoulders, crossing them in front so they hung at each side. She stretched to reach the flashlight, then eased herself out onto the ledge.

Icy water sloshed around her ankles. The bags jostled her until she nearly lost her balance. She steadied them, then poked the flashlight into her pocket so both hands were free.

As she felt her way for the next step, a wave slammed hard against her.

Chapter Ten

The blood pounded in Jessie's temples. Another wave spewed over her legs, catching the bottoms of the plastic bags. She felt the pull and leaned closer into the cliff as she yanked up on the cords. Why hadn't she told Allie to hold the other light for her?

"Allie!" she yelled.

The crashing waves blotted out her voice.

Step, shuffle. The next wave fell short. Surely she was almost across. She clung to handholds formed by the pocked rocks. If only she could hold the flashlight, but, stuck down in her pocket, it shone straight up in the air.

At last her hand found an edge that curved, and she breathed a sigh of relief. But was she across? In the darkness she couldn't even see the sandy beach. Two more steps. Her foot found the end of the ledge!

Now, if she could just find the step-down rocks. And if the water hadn't covered them.

Suddenly a light cut through the darkness.

"Jessie!" Allie cried.

In the beam of light, water swirled around the rock and raced several yards up the beach. No way to tell how deep it was. Stay calm, she told herself. The seventh wave. Was that what Pop had told her? If you get caught by the tide, count the waves. Every seventh is lower.

One. She watched the swirling white foam roll in, then recede. Two. That one was higher! Allie moved the light, following the wave far up on the sand. Which one is the seventh? Maybe she should take a chance and wade in. Three. It rolled in and met the outgoing water. The fourth wave came only to the rock and eddied around it.

Now! She must go now! She flew off the rocks and jumped to the sand. But before she could run, another wave swirled above her knees and she had to catch herself against the cliff. Grit filled her shoes and receding water drained the sand from beneath her feet, stealing her power, threatening to suck her out to sea.

She sloshed upward with effort. One step. Two. A fury sounded behind her, deafening! She pulled herself to solid sand and ran.

"Whew!" She gulped for air, from fear or struggling or maybe both. She dropped the two bags on the sand and stood a moment getting her breath. Her legs felt like Toady's gummy-worm candies.

Allie grabbed both bags and dragged them up the beach.

"Where's Toady?" Jessie asked.

"I'm here. Jessie, I'm tired. Can we go home now?" He sounded sleepy.

Jessie's feet felt like heavy rocks as she plodded behind Allie.

When they reached a flat boulder, well back from the surf, she saw that the kids had carried everything to safety.

Jessie sat down and pulled Toady to her. "I want to tell you something," she said.

"I don't want to. I wanna go home!" He jerked away from her.

He'd guessed earlier, Jessie told herself, but he didn't want to believe it. He's got to understand.

"Toady, we can't go home." She had to say it. "If we go back, those people will take us away. We have to stay here until Mom and Pop can get things straightened out."

"I don't believe you! Pop wouldn't let them take us!" he said, near tears.

"Toady, it's true," Allie said. "It's really true. That's what the man said this afternoon. You heard."

Toady stared at them. The eerie light showed the scared look on his face. "What're we gonna do?"

"We'll stay here for a few days." This time when she reached for him, he came to her and stood against her. "Come on, now. We'll get these wet clothes off and get into bed."

There was no way they could climb the cliff tonight. They'd have to sleep here on the sand. Or up on the rocks at the end of the cove.

She decided on the sand. It was softer and still held some of the day's warmth. Besides, she couldn't go another step.

"Take off your wet clothes," Jessie ordered. "We'll

dry them tomorrow." She spread out the two sleeping bags, thankful to find them dry. "Allie, we'll sleep together. We lost one of the bags." She brushed sand off Toady and stuffed him down into one bag. Allie slipped out of her wet things, pulled on dry pajamas, and disappeared into the other.

Jessie's clothes clung to her, cold and gritty, as she peeled them off. The dry pajamas felt as warm as if they'd just come from the dryer. It's because I'm so cold, she mused. Snuggling in with Allie, she shivered at the sudden warmth. Tiredness consumed her until her whole body felt weak.

They would need to be up early tomorrow. And hide before anyone came looking for them. Tomorrow. It's already tomorrow, she thought.

Chapter Eleven

*T*he shrill "scree, scree, scree" of seagulls tangled with softer "shuuushing" sounds. Jessie opened her eyes to gray sky. It was all true. She hadn't just dreamed it.

Suddenly the enormity of what she'd done felt like a whale landing on her chest. Would they be all right? Would they have enough food? How long would they have to stay hidden?

She looked at her watch. Eight o'clock. She counted on her fingers. *Only six hours until those people would be back.* To take them away. We have to make it, she told herself. We have to.

She scooted out of the sleeping bag into the chilly air.

"Jessie, I have to go to the bathroom," Toady said.

"Go over there behind that rock," she told him. That was something else they'd have to think about. She'd planned to dig a latrine like Pop had shown them on camping trips. But dig with what? She hadn't thought of bringing a shovel and couldn't have carried it if she had.

She rummaged in the packs and found a pair of jeans for each of them. Too bad they hadn't brought a second pair of shoes. Still, the sun would dry them in no time.

Toady came running back, his stout, tanned body pounding across the sand. "Hey, Jessie," he shouted. "Is this where we're gonna stay?"

"Not exactly," Jessie told him. She pulled on her jeans and buttoned them. Then she bent and peeked at Allie. Allie was the late sleeper in the family, and Mom always said she needed more rest than the others. It seemed early here in the deep shadow of overhanging cliffs, but Mom and Pop would have been up at least two hours. *They already knew they were gone!*

Toady ran down to the water's edge. Waves splashed high on the rocky ledge where they'd crossed last night, and white foam rolled halfway up the beach. A dozen seagulls stood on the shiny, wet sand, watching as though expecting a handout. The gulls' sharp cries and the water pulling at the sand were the only sounds. Peaceful, Jessie thought.

The roar of a plane shattered the stillness as it flew above their heads and disappeared over the ocean.

"Hey, look!" cried Toady, running toward her and waving at the plane.

Jessie grabbed him and yanked him into the shadow of the rocks. Too late, she thought, if they're looking for us.

"What's the matter?" Toady cried, as though sensing her fear.

"We don't want anybody to see us," she said sternly.

"Oh, yeah, I forgot."

Allie sat up, awakened by the noise. "What's

wrong?" she groaned. Shivering, she dragged her bag across the sand.

"Stay here in case that plane comes back," said Jessie. She handed Allie dry jeans and a shirt. The dampness could be bad for her asthma.

Jessie listened and peered out over the sea, but there was no sign of the plane. Maybe no one saw them after all. The towering headlands at either end of the cove did give them some protection. Besides, maybe it was just one of the whale-watching planes that took tourists out over the ocean.

"I'm hungry," Toady complained.

"Wait a bit," Jessie told him.

Hunched into the folds of her sleeping bag, Allie squatted on the rock, shivering. "What'll we do now, Jessie?"

"We have to climb up there." She pointed to the steep sand dune that spilled down between rocky bluffs. From here the tree was hidden from view.

"What's up there?" Toady asked.

"A place where we can stay."

"Is it a house?" Allie asked.

"No, we're camping out, remember."

"Can I be the leader again?" Toady asked, putting on his Adventure Man hat.

"Sure."

"Can we have a bonfire?" Allie asked.

Jessie shook her head. "We don't have any matches." She'd forgotten. Dumb to have forgotten matches.

"Well, how'll we cook?" Toady demanded.

"We won't. It's like a picnic."

Maybe they should eat something before climbing the hill.

She took the jar of peanut butter and a box of crackers from her pack. "Here," she told Allie and Toady, as she unscrewed the lid and ripped off the foil seal. "Use a cracker to scoop some out." They'd eat more later, but this would hold them for now.

Toady grabbed a handful of crackers, dipped each into peanut butter, and gobbled them down.

Allie carefully smoothed peanut butter over her cracker with one finger while Toady dug in for more.

Jessie rolled the sleeping bags and crammed them back into their sacks.

"Everybody grab something and start climbing," she told them. "It'll take two or three trips. Okay, are we ready?" she asked.

"I'm still eating," Allie said.

"Well, hurry. We need to get out of sight."

"How come?" Toady asked.

"Remember?" Allie said around a mouthful.

"Oh, yeah," Toady said. He ran partway up the dune, then slid back down, laughing.

Jessie rolled up the wet clothing they'd worn last night, shouldered a sleeping bag, and picked up the smaller pack. She moved slowly, staying with Allie, who carried the other sleeping bag. Toady raced ahead, then came sliding back, sand clinging to his clothing.

"Look, I'm skiing," he called.

Let him have fun, Jessie told herself, despite her impatience. Besides, he needed to run off some energy.

"Follow Adventure Man!" he cried, digging his heels into the sand as he started up the hill once more.

It had been cool by the water, but the sun already burned down on the dune. Halfway up, Jessie felt smothered by the sweat running down her face. Hot sand spilled around her bare feet, pulling her backward. When she looked back over the ocean, she saw no sign of the plane. Maybe it wasn't a search plane after all. But the Coast Guard might send a helicopter. Hurry, hurry, she thought, walking faster. Get everything out of sight.

"Jessie, I can't keep up," Allie complained.

"Allie, I have to get these things to the top and go back for the rest. Can't you climb by yourself? I'll be where you can see me."

"I guess," Allie answered, sounding close to tears.

Jessie moved up the cliff, turning her feet sideways to get a better foothold.

"Look, Jessie, there's a house up there," Toady said when they reached the top.

"I know, but there's no one home," she answered, as she stuffed things beneath some bushes. "Now, let's go get the rest."

Toady slid on his seat almost to the bottom, paddling his legs to propel himself over slow spots. Jessie laughed as she watched him. It looked like such fun that for a moment she was tempted to try it, too.

Allie looked like a tiny brown doll surrounded by golden sand. She'd hardly moved at all.

Her medicine! Jessie snatched up her wet jacket and dug into the pocket. She dropped to the ground, relieved, when she found the bottles safe.

Going back down the dune, she stopped beside Allie. Was she breathing too heavily? Was it that horrible wheezing? "Leave that bag for Toady," Jessie told her. "Rest whenever you need to. Just go slow."

Jessie ran the rest of the way, feeling as if she might tumble headlong at any moment.

"I can carry the food," Toady said, tugging to lift the heavy pack.

"No, go help Allie. Carry that sleeping bag."

"Are we gonna live in that house?" Toady asked.

"Nope."

"Then where'll we live?"

"You'll see. It's a surprise."

"Secret, you mean," he grumbled as they started back up the hill.

It was slow going with the heavy pack. Halfway up she heard a plane once again. Not close—yet. Her heart pounded in her ears as she looked around the bare dune.

"Allie! Toady!" she yelled. When they turned, she motioned to a cluster of rocks at the edge of the dune and ran in that direction. Both children followed.

"Why'd we come over here?" Toady demanded.

"The plane. I think it's coming back," Jessie said.

"They might be looking for us. We'll have to wait here until it's gone." At least it was shady here.

Allie's face looked more peaked than ever, but after they'd rested her breathing evened out. So it wasn't her asthma.

"It's too high for a search plane," Jessie said, after the plane had gone back out over the ocean. Once they had reached the tree and had all their things hidden she could relax. Maybe she'd even climb to the top and read.

Instead of going back to the center of the dune, they followed its rock-strewn edge almost to the top. It was easier walking there because the ground was solid, although the climb was steeper. Jessie stopped to catch her breath several times, and at last she took Allie's hand to urge her on.

Toady lagged behind. Just before they reached the top he threw down his Adventure Man hat and glared at Jessie.

"I'm tired," he said. His face was red, and his rumpled hair was wet with sweat.

"Just a little farther, Toady."

"I'm not goin'."

"Look, you have to." Annoyance made her voice sharp.

"I don't."

"Toady, pick up your things and come on!"

He stood with arms folded stiffly.

Jessie grabbed up the sleeping bag and started off.

"Just stay there, then," she said. "Let them find you

and take you back to Sherrill!" As soon as she said the words she was sorry.

Allie let out a little cry. "No, Jessie, no!" She ran to Toady and began urging him on.

Now I've done it, Jessie thought. The bags on her back felt heavy, but her insides felt heavier.

She stopped and gazed up at the tree. Her tree. Her secret place. It looked as goldy-green as the day, several months ago, when she'd first seen it. When she'd discovered the rock ledge and climbed the dune that first time.

Sunlight had played across the bronze leaves as the breeze stirred them, and for a moment an opening appeared—secret, mysterious. She'd felt a swelling excitement and curiosity, as though the tree had given her a sign.

Its leaves, like golden fingers, had beckoned her beneath branches that swooped nearly to the ground, and the inside had felt like a great, shimmering room. Surely there had never been a tree like it anywhere before.

Chapter Twelve

$\mathcal{J}$essie ran the last few yards and slipped beneath the branches of the chinquapin tree. Staring upward into the cool dimness, she savored this last moment alone. Her high seat was touched by streaks of sunlight. Closing her eyes, she remembered other days, sitting there, reading, dreaming.

Never again would it be her own secret place. Allie and Toady would invade her quiet place. She dropped the heavy bags and stroked a smooth limb with her fingers. Still . . .

"Jessie! Where'd you go?" Allie's voice bordered on panic.

"In here," she called. Both children scuttled beneath the branches and stood looking about.

"Wow!" Toady said. "Is this where we're gonna stay? It's the biggest tree I ever saw! I never was inside a tree before."

Jessie laughed. "Well, it's not really inside." Still, it was, she guessed. Both children stood empty-handed. Why couldn't they carry something in?

"Can we climb it?" Toady asked.

"We have to bring our stuff in here." She'd just go get it all herself. She tried not to show her annoyance.

"I'm hungry," Toady said.

For the first time Jessie realized how empty she felt. She hadn't eaten anything down on the beach. But what if the plane came back? Or a helicopter searching for them?

"We'll eat in a few minutes." Thinking of the bacon and eggs Mom sometimes fixed for breakfast made her stomach lurch.

"I'm thirsty, too."

"Have to wait." She ducked back out into the bright sunlight.

Hesitating, she stared at the empty windows of the house on the hill. What if somebody's there? Mom said Miss Bjorset was in Europe. But what if someone else . . . She sighed and hefted their things to her shoulder. She should spread their wet clothes on the grass to dry, but that was too risky. She scooted everything beneath the low-growing branches and stepped inside.

Crackers and cans and bowls and peanut butter lay strewn about, and Toady was digging in the backpack.

"Toady! What are you doing?"

"I'm looking for a box of cereal and some milk."

"You won't find them. Put that stuff back. No, I'll do it myself. Now stay out of things." How does Mom always stay so calm?

Moments later Toady called, "Look, Jessie." He hung upside down from a low branch, a half-peeled banana in one hand. While she watched, he swung himself back up and cradled the limb against his face. "Jessie, it's like the tree's hugging me."

Jessie sighed. Funny little kid. One minute he's a pest and the next he says something like that. She'd felt that way sometimes, too.

"Can I climb way up?"

"Sure," she said with a sigh. "You can help me hang our wet clothes on the limbs."

Toady poked the rest of the banana into his mouth, then went hand-over-hand upward.

"Hang everything on inside branches where nobody can see them."

When they'd finished, Toady reached for a cluster of spiny burrs. "What're these?" he asked, then yelled "Ouch!" and let them drop to the ground.

Jessie laughed and picked one from a branch. Carefully, she pressed open the burr and removed the small nut. "Crack it when you get down. They're good to eat."

Toady swung from limb to limb. Like a monkey, Jessie thought.

"Look, Allie," he cried as he came down. "Nuts! We can eat them." He found a rock and cracked one. "They're awful little, though." He handed a nut to Allie. "There's millions of 'em," he said looking up, "but they're stickery."

Jessie stood wondering what to do next when Toady demanded, "I want something else to eat. I'm starving."

"Just wait."

"Then can I go down to the beach?"

"No! Be quiet, can't you?"

"Don't be so bossy!" he shouted as he disappeared beyond the low-hanging branches.

Jessie glared after him, hating that word. Why couldn't he cooperate? Was this going to work, or would it be a hassle the whole time?

"I'll help," Allie offered. "Just tell me what to do."

Jessie forced a smile. "Thanks, Allie. Mostly, I'm trying to figure some things out. Since we lost a sleeping bag, I think we should spread the other two flat, then cover up with our jackets. If it's cold at night we can sleep in our jeans and shirts."

"Want me to do it?"

But Jessie hesitated. "Maybe we should leave them rolled during the day."

"Okay." Allie picked up one bag at a time and stacked them against the tree's trunk.

The air felt stuffy here under the tree. Jessie gathered her long red hair with one hand and pulled it back. She wished she had something to tie it.

"Hey, Jessie," Toady called, bursting through the branches at the back of the tree. "Look, there's a big sandpile out here."

Jessie peered out. "Wind probably blows it up here," she told him.

"I'm hot," Toady complained, already stripping off his shirt. "How come we don't have any shorts?"

"We didn't have room," Jessie told him.

"Well, I'm not wearing these hot jeans," he said as he pulled them off.

"Shorts would be cooler," Jessie mused. "We could

cut off our pajamas and make shorts. Allie, you got scissors in your sewing?"

Allie dug out a tiny pair of scissors and began nibbling at the cloth. "It's awful slow," she said.

"Golly, that's lots cooler," Jessie said when she put hers on. "Thanks, Allie."

Allie held up a pajama top. "I'll cut off the sleeves so we'll have cool tops, too."

When Allie finished, Jessie picked up the cut-off legs and sleeves. "We can use these to wash up and dry on. And I know what else." She tore a strip from one of the pajama sleeves and tied her hair into a ponytail.

"I'm thirsty," Toady complained.

"There's a faucet below the house," Jessie said "I've seen it from the top of the tree."

She dipped a cracker into the open jar of peanut butter and popped it into her mouth. Then she dug out two plastic bowls for water. "Toady, where's your hat? We need a good leader now."

Stepping outside she glanced again toward the house and drew in her breath sharply. For the briefest moment she'd seen—but what had she seen? The windows weren't the kind you could see through from outside. They looked like mirrors set into the weathered, angular framework. Still, she'd seen—or sensed—something. Was someone inside? Watching?

"Where's the faucet?" Allie asked.

Jessie hesitated. Should they stay hidden? But if someone were watching they'd have seen them already.

"Jessie!"

"This way, I think," Jessie said, walking up the hill toward the house. But she'd gone only a short distance when a tall thicket of salal brush blocked her way. Its pretty, round leaves looked soft, but Jessie knew its twigs were as scratchy as briars. They'd have to find a way around it.

Toady, Adventure Man hat pulled tight on his head, plunged into a clump. "Follow *Adventure Man*," he yelled.

"Toady, I think Adventure Man will have to find another way."

Jessie skirted a few small clumps but each time came to a dead end.

"Are there snakes here?" Allie asked in a small voice.

"Of course not," Jessie said quickly, although a trickle of fear raced through her. "They're probably all out in that field." Why did Allie have to bring that up? It wasn't that Jessie was afraid of snakes, not like they were poisonous or anything, but she didn't like them to startle her.

"I found a way," Toady called, his voice muffled by the brush between them.

"Look," he said when they found him.

A narrow path, barely visible in the grass, wound into the thick brush.

"Probably an animal's trail," Jessie said, following Toady and Allie. The path twisted and turned, sometimes arching so low they had to duck down, but always leading deeper into the thicket.

"It's like a maze," Allie said. "Like the ones in my puzzle book."

Suddenly, Toady cried, "Hey, I can't go no farther."

They had come into a wide grassy area completely surrounded by tall salal.

"And look." He pointed. The ground was covered with deer droppings. The grass was mashed down as though the animals had slept there.

"Is it a bear?" Allie asked fearfully.

"Just deer," Jessie told them. The salal formed a hidden room.

"Wow!" Toady cried. "Can this be my secret hide-out? Nobody'd ever find me here."

Jessie smiled. "Sure, Toady, but we'll have to find another way to the water faucet."

After much backtracking and picking their way through and around smaller clumps of brush, they finally came out just below what looked like a long-neglected garden. The faucet stood at one corner and beside it was a large square wooden box, an old fish box like the kind Pop used in his greenhouses. Probably for setting things on or storing hoses and sprinklers, Jessie decided. Green paint flaked from the wooden boards, but Jessie made out black letters: Harbor Fish Co.

"Where's Toady?" Allie asked.

Jessie stood still and surveyed the slope that led to the house. "Toady," she called. "Where the heck has he gone?"

Suddenly he popped from behind the box and

shouted, "Adventure Man!" Grinning, he said, "Scared you, huh?" He bent down and peered inside the box. "I was going to hide there, but I thought you'd see me," he said. Then he practically stood on his head to drink at the faucet.

"Use this to wash your face," Jessie said, holding out a wet sleeve from her pajamas. "It'll help cool you off."

They took turns drinking, then filled the bowls and started back, Jessie helping Allie maneuver through the thick brush while Toady disappeared. Why did he have to be so pesky? And why didn't he stay with them?

"I hate this!" Allie cried. "That brush scratches. We should have waited to put on shorts."

Jessie's shoulders sagged. Her arms and legs were scratched, too, and her hair and neck felt prickly from heat and dust. And where had Toady gone? Why was everything such a hassle?

"Jessie! I found a trail, a good one down by the edge of the cliff." Toady cried, bursting from behind a bush. "And it comes out right at the sand pile! Come on, I'll show you."

Jessie sighed and plodded after him.

Toady ran on ahead. When they reached the tree, he came flying from beneath its branches. "Beat you!" he cried, his mouth filled with crackers.

"No wonder we didn't find the trail," Jessie said, "It was hidden behind that spruce tree." She indicated a towering evergreen that stood beyond the smooth mound of sand.

"Yeah, and look at the good hidey place." Toady dropped onto the sand and slithered beneath dense, green branches and was soon hidden.

"This can be our back door," Allie said.

Jessie grinned at her sister. "Yeah," she said. "I'm glad you found that trail, Toady."

He wriggled back into sight. "Ouch, that tree's got stickery needles." Still, he was obviously pleased with himself.

Toady and Allie flopped down in the sand and began smoothing it with their hands. "Jessie, this can be our patio," Allie said, sifting sand through her fingers.

Jessie grinned, then took the water inside and set it down. "Right now we need to . . ." she began. She picked up the cracker box. Empty. "Toady!" she called, as she poked her head through the branches. "Did you eat all of these?"

He nodded. "I was starving."

Jessie sighed and dropped the box. Couldn't blame him, they hadn't eaten much.

"Jessie," Allie asked, "how will we know when we can go back home?"

"I haven't figured that out yet."

"I could go back and ask Pop," Toady volunteered.

"No, Toady! You stay here—*right here* close to us. Understand?" She couldn't have him getting any such ideas.

"Uh-huh."

"Get your things and play," she told him.

"Can I slide down the sand hill to the beach?"

"No, Toady. Now go do something. But stay hidden."

How long would their food last? she wondered. She opened her pack and took out the apples, bananas, the cans of tuna and other meats, and the package of hot dogs.

Suddenly the deafening sound of engines whisked her words away.

A helicopter! *Where was Toady?*

She rushed from the tree and called to him, but the noise drowned her words. Besides, the copter was already out over the ocean. Toady stood gazing after it.

"Toady! I told you to stay hidden!" she yelled. "Why don't you listen?"

"But I wanted to see it. Besides, I was under that bush."

"Well, I hope he didn't see you," Allie scolded. "You heard what Jessie said."

Toady made a face. "She's too bossy."

Jessie turned away and slammed her hand against the tree's broad trunk.

Chapter Thirteen

$\mathscr{T}$he helicopter did not return, but Jessie insisted they stay hidden just in case. She took out the package of hot dogs, now thawed, and unwrapped them. The salty smell tugged at her stomach, making her realize her own hunger.

"Are we having hot dogs for breakfast?" Toady asked.

"No, silly, it's already afternoon. We need to eat these first because they'll spoil. And save the canned stuff for later."

They wolfed them down. Then each ate an apple, washing everything down with water.

Jessie was surprised at how much stronger she felt after eating. Carefully, she put the rest of their food back into her bag.

"Let's keep everything packed," she told them. Why did she feel so uneasy?

Allie sat embroidering tiny red and yellow flowers on a bright turquoise cloth, while Toady played with his cars and some stickmen he'd made from twigs.

"Jessie," Allie said, "what if Mom and Pop can't change those people's mind? What then?"

No, no, I don't want to think that way. Still, she should try to answer, for herself as well as Allie.

"If I was older," she said, "old enough so they'd let me take care of all of us. . . ."

Allie remained silent. "I could do it. You know I have. Remember back in Portland?"

"I know, Jessie."

"If it wasn't so far to a city maybe we could go there. Maybe Coos Bay, but it's a long ways. It's easier to hide in a city."

Sometimes Sherrill wouldn't come home for days at a time. One time when she had left them alone and the next-door neighbor kept checking on them, they told her Sherrill was sick. When the woman kept bugging them, Jessie had bundled some things together and they had gone out onto the streets. They'd stayed in an all-night laundry. It was warm there, and for some reason no attendant showed up. The next night they'd hidden in a small mall, slinking in behind some old counters and shelves where remodeling was going on. But by the next day Toady was filthy and ran around, attracting attention. They'd returned to the apartment and found Sherrill asleep. She'd never even asked where they'd been.

"We managed that time," Jessie said.

Allie had put aside her needlework and sat on her haunches, scratching lines in the sand with a stick. "But I was scared," she almost whispered.

Jessie looked at her for a long moment. "We all were, Allie."

"I wasn't," Toady boasted.

Allie laughed. "You were little, only a baby."

"Was I, Jessie?"

"You were maybe three."

"But I wasn't scared," he insisted.

"Toady, you don't even remember."

He stood up, scowling. "But I wouldn't a-been scared if I did."

"Toady, mellow out," Jessie said.

"We could find an empty house and live there," he said. "You could take care of us then."

Jessie drew in a long breath and let it out. "You can't just find a house, Toady."

"Why not? That one up there's empty."

"Houses belong to somebody. Besides, there's other things. How would we buy food, and . . ."

"You could find a way, if you wanted to." He stomped away.

"He's so stubborn when he gets an idea," Allie said.

Jessie met her sister's eyes and smiled. It felt good that Toady thought she could care for them. She sighed. She wasn't even sure about that.

"We won't go to a city, will we?" Allie asked.

Jessie sat thinking. It was true it hadn't worked before. "There are places to hide in a city. And food."

"Yuck!" Allie cried. "I hated eating garbage!"

"Allie, it wasn't garbage. I waited in that restaurant where I went to the bathroom, and that family got up and left all those hamburgers with only a bite or two out of each one. No one was around, so I just gathered them in napkins and took them. The waitress thought I was part of their family."

"Well, it would have been garbage."

"Look, Allie, let's not worry about that until we

have to. Right now we just have to keep on for a day or so and hope."

Toady came back and flopped down nearby. He picked up his stickmen and marched a man up to Allie's Barbies, making guttural, hissing noises. "We're gonna take you away!"

"Don't," Allie screamed. "Jessie! Make him stop."

"I don't have to!"

"Jessieee!"

Jessie closed her eyes and squeezed her lips together. "Stop fighting!" she yelled.

Both kids stared at her. Had she yelled too loud? What if someone heard her?

She looked upward to the splotches of blue sky showing through golden leaves. Her peaceful perch beckoned. If only . . .

"Hey, want to climb all the way to the top?" she asked.

"Yeah!" Toady cried, jumping up, his stickmen flying.

Allie looked frightened.

"You don't have to," Jessie told her.

"I'll go just a little ways."

Toady scrambled halfway to the top while Allie clung awkwardly to the first limb, her body rigid when Jessie tried to help her.

"You're only a few feet from the ground," Jessie told her.

"Can I sit here and watch?" Allie asked.

"Sure."

"Ho, Adventure Man!" Toady cried, swinging out on a limb, then finding the next with his bare toes.

"Wow!" Toady cried when they reached the place where the limbs formed a seat.

"It's our crow's nest. I can watch for pirates!"

"Good idea," Jessie said, surprised that she didn't mind sharing this place with her brother. She parted branches and peered out over the ocean. Fishing boats, their tall masts stabbing the air, were silhouetted against a sky now glowing pink and orange. Soon sunset would turn it to deep purple and orange. They'd been here almost a whole day already. She wondered what Mom and Pop were doing. Were they out looking for them? For a moment she closed her eyes, longing to be with them.

"Jessie, somebody's up there," Toady whispered.

Jessie turned quickly and peered through the branches. A tall boy disappeared around the corner of the house.

"Is he lookin' for us?" Toady asked, echoing Jessie's thoughts.

"Shhhh." She remembered her earlier feeling of being watched.

The loud sputtering of a motor startled her so she nearly lost her balance. Then, realizing it was only a lawn mower, she let her breath out slowly. They watched the boy walk back and forth behind the mower. It was scary to see him so clearly, to see his brown hair fall over his forehead, then flip back as he jerked his head up. The mingled smells of gasoline and newly cut grass drifted to them.

She crouched lower among the branches and motioned to Toady, who slid down beside her.

The boy stopped and wiped his face with his sleeve, then stood tall and seemed to look right at them.

Toady stiffened and drew back.

"He can't see us," Jessie said. "Stay here and watch, okay? But keep down."

We need a plan just in case, she told herself.

Allie stood, looking scared. "Is somebody coming?" she asked.

"I hope not," Jessie said. She was glad everything was still packed. But where would they go? How could they hide? They didn't even dare step outside the tree.

Unless . . . The back door. She remembered Toady sliding out of sight beneath the tall spruce.

"Come down, Toady. Quick. Here, Allie, take these." Quickly she bundled their stuff together and headed for the back door. "We'll hide under the spruce tree, just in case," she told them as she smoothed the sand to hide their footprints.

Toady dropped to the ground and grabbed the things Jessie held out to him, then slithered out of sight.

"It feels like a porcupine," Allie complained. "Ouch!"

"That's what will keep us hidden," Jessie told her, but jerked her own arm back as bristly needles jabbed her shoulder.

"No talking," she whispered.

"How'll we know when it's safe?" Allie asked softly.

"Shhhh."

As her eyes became accustomed to the dimness, Jessie realized she could see plainly where the path led beneath the chinquapin tree.

After what seemed hours, Jessie heard a twig snap. Allie grabbed her hand, and almost at once she saw boots walking toward them. No one made a sound. The boots stopped, and Jessie held her breath. Could he see them? What if he stooped and peered in?

Instead, the boots moved on to their tree. For a moment a boy, slightly older than Jessie, stood holding back the branches. He was tall, with brown hair, and wore jeans and a shirt. He disappeared beneath the tree.

The clothes they'd hung on the limbs! She'd forgotten about those in their rush to hide. Don't let him look up, Jessie prayed silently.

Moments later he came out and stood so close to Jessie's face that she could smell the cut grass still clinging to his boots. Silence hung about them. . . .

After a bit he turned and slowly walked back up the trail.

No one moved for a long time.

Goosebumps stood out on Jessie's arms, and she felt shaky inside when she and the younger children finally scooted through the sand into the late afternoon sunshine.

Toady shinnied up the tree to see what was happening at the house.

"Don't see nobody," he called down in a loud whisper.

"You think he's gone?" Allie asked in a small voice as she chewed on the tail of her shirt.

"Probably," Jessie said, hoping Allie couldn't hear the pounding of her heart.

Feeling as if she were a robot, she set the packs down.

She peeked into the food bag. Only the cans of tuna and sausages, some apples and two bananas, and the rest of the jar of peanut butter remained.

Last night she'd thought she had lots of food. Now it was almost gone. Nothing was working out the way she'd planned.

They'd had hot dogs earlier. Well, they could eat apples and peanut butter tonight.

They sat at the cliff's edge, eating their meager supper and watching the sunset that transformed the whole sky to flame. Below them, the ocean shusshed softly. Crickets and other insects set up a scratchy concert. A bird scolded from a bush. All seemed peaceful.

Jessie spread the sleeping bags before darkness fell.

"Jessie, do you think that boy will come back?" Allie asked as they lay watching darkness close in.

"I hope not," Jessie said. "Maybe when he didn't find anything . . ." Her own doubts kept her from finishing.

After they were in bed, Jessie tried to remember how many minus tides showed in her tide book. Tomorrow at least, but it might be the last one for a while. Then they'd be stuck here for days.

Chapter Fourteen

Jessie sat huddled against the tree trunk, fully dressed and snuggled into her coat. She'd gotten up hours ago, dozed, then wakened. Now light filtered through the leaves above. A bird twittered. Something scuttled away in the bushes behind her. Bits of sky above her head glowed pink. With her fingernail she made a mark beside today's date in her tide book. It was important to keep track of the days.

Allie was right about that time in the city. They couldn't stay in one place for fear of being noticed. Besides, cold rains would start soon. And school. Three children who should be in school were sure to attract attention.

At least she'd made one decision. It might be risky, but she'd have to go back to the house tonight to get enough food to last a few more days. She'd checked the tide. Only a minus 0.9 and low at 4:07 a.m. But maybe she could cross by 3:30.

Sudden thrashing in the bushes outside brought her to her feet.

"Who's in there?" someone asked, and goosebumps stood out on her arms. Allie raised up, her eyes wide.

"What's that?" Toady cried.

Jessie parted the branches, her heart racing. Standing a few feet away was the boy they'd seen yesterday!

He stood taller than Jessie, and for a moment they stared at one another.

"What do you want?" she finally asked, trying to keep her voice steady.

"Can I come in?"

Uncertainly, Jessie stepped aside.

The boy frowned and stepped into the tree room. "What's all this? Trespassers?"

"No, no," Jessie stammered, trying to think what to say—or do, for that matter. "We—we're just camping out." She raised her chin defiantly.

"On Miss Bjorset's place? You don't have permission." Steady gray eyes looked straight at her.

"How do you know?"

"I just know. I come over and check things and cut her grass while she's away. She would have said if . . ."

"She probably forgot," Jessie said quickly. "She was in such a rush to go."

The boy studied them for a moment. "Maybe," he said doubtfully. "Who are you anyway? Where do you live?"

Jessie gulped and avoided his eyes by stooping and saying to Allie and Toady, "Better get up." She was glad she'd thrown the sleeping bag over them when she crawled out, so the boy would think they needed to get dressed. "Would you mind waiting outside?" she said as calmly as possible.

"Sure. No problem."

Maybe he'd just go away and leave them alone. But she knew better. She waited, trying to think what to do. "Roll the sleeping bags," she told Allie and Toady before raising the branches and inviting him back inside.

"How long you been here?" the boy asked at once.

"Oh, a day or so."

She turned and dug into one of the packs just to look busy, all the time wondering what would happen now. "What's your name?"

"Jasper," the boy said. "Jasper Fredrickson."

Jessie looked at him. "That's a funny name."

"Yeah. My mom named me that 'cause she thought it would sound good for a lawyer or a doctor."

"You're going to be a doctor or lawyer?" Jessie asked.

"Naw. Too boring. But I don't tell Mom that." He grinned. A friendly grin, Jessie decided.

"What then?" Jessie asked, mostly to keep the conversation away from them until she could figure out what to say.

He placed his hands behind him on a low limb and hoisted himself onto it before answering.

He's older than me, Jessie decided. Maybe sixteen.

"A foreign news correspondent."

"Really?" Jessie said with interest. "You've already decided? You *know* what you'll do when you grow up?"

"That's right. Here, picture this." He swung both hands in front of him and said, sounding like a newscaster on TV, "We now go to Jasper Fredrickson in South Africa, covering this story live, or . . ." He paused and pretended to change channels. "And now to Banko, where Jasper Fredrickson has the latest developments." He dropped his arms and grinned.

"Golly," Jessie sounded impressed.

He looked at them a moment, then said, "Or how about this? Jasper Fredrickson brings you the latest on the missing Cloud children."

"Oh!" Jessie felt her breath go out and the blood drain from her face.

Jasper sat watching them. "Guessed right, huh?"

Allie's hand slipped into Jessie's.

"So, are you going to tell?" Jessie hoped her voice didn't sound as shaky as she felt.

"I might." He sat watching them. "And then, I might not."

"Well, if you're going to, go do it!" she yelled. "Don't sit there playing your games and looking so smart!" She felt tears sting behind her lids and raised her chin, shaking all over with fury.

"Hey." He slid off the branch and stepped closer. "Don't fly off at me. I won't tell. But what's the deal, anyway? Why'd you run away? How come you're hiding out here?"

"Because those people want to send us back to Sherrill, that's why," Allie cried.

"You mean your mother?"

"Huh!" Allie exploded, as she folded skinny brown arms across her chest.

"Well, she is your mother, isn't she?"

"She doesn't want us," Allie said, glowering at him.

"She just wants to get welfare money."

He stood, thoughtful, listening.

"It wasn't good living with her," Jessie said, surprised at how calm she felt.

"What did she do? Beat you?"

Somehow Jessie didn't want to admit that. "Sometimes," she said hesitantly. "It was other things, too."

"She fed us cooked rats!" Allie said.

"Cooked rats?"

"It wasn't really," Jessie put in. "It was some kind of chicken. But Allie asked what it was, and Sherrill told her she'd killed some of the big rats that ran through our apartment."

"And she laughed when I threw up all over," Allie said.

"Ugh!" Jasper made a face.

"How long have you known we were here?" Jessie asked.

He gave her a sheepish glance. "I saw you yesterday. Hiding under that tree."

He paused. "I decided to come back today and see if you were still here. Then, last night I heard about three missing children. Jessie, Allie, and Toady. Right?"

"You were watching from the windows!" Jessie remembered how she'd felt when they went for water.

He nodded.

"You saw us hiding," Toady blurted. "How come you didn't say something yesterday?"

Jasper shrugged. "I've watched your sister before, you know."

"You spied on me?" Jessie cried. And all the time she'd thought her place so secret.

"Not spied. I saw you climb the tree and sit there reading lots of times. Miss Bjorset spotted you first. She called me to the window one day and laughed as she said, 'See, I have a red-headed bird in my tree.' She told me not to bother you as long as you just came to the tree."

Jessie felt her face burning with embarrassment.

"Then yesterday I saw the three of you go to the faucet below the garden. I was inside watering her plants."

"Did you know we were hiding?" Toady asked.

Jasper grinned. "Not at first. But, when I saw all those clothes draped over the tree limbs . . ."

Jessie caught her breath.

". . . and when I came back out I saw the tree had grown feet." He grinned. "I had to find out what was going on. You know, because Miss Bjorset trusts me. To take care of things."

"So, what now?" Jessie demanded.

He looked directly at her. "I don't know." It was almost a question.

"We're only stayin' till Pop works things out," Toady put in.

"Look, most people in town are rooting for you. They want those people to let you stay. But that might not happen. Right?"

"Maybe." Jessie said.

"So, I guess if you need a few days . . ."

"You won't tell?" Toady demanded.

"You okay? Got something to eat?"

"We brought lots of food," Toady boasted. Jessie did not correct him. After tonight they'd have plenty. After she went back to the house.

"Look, I live just down the road. On the other side of that ridge of fir trees at the top of the hill. I'll come by every day and check on you. Just in case you need something."

"Thanks," Jessie said. "Pop'll have things straightened out in a few days. And we won't bother anything. We won't go to the house—just the faucet for water."

"Deal," Jasper said. "Hey, Toady, these your cars?"

The two knelt in the sand, and Jessie watched while Jasper played with Toady.

After a bit Toady jumped up and said, "I'm hungry."

"Get an apple," Jessie told him. She couldn't let Jasper know how low their food supply was. Besides, after tonight they'd be just fine.

She walked out to the pile of sand, where the sun warmed her.

Jasper followed and sat down cross-legged. He dipped his big hands into the sand and let it sift through his fingers. "Have you plans beyond here?" he asked. "If things don't work out?"

She couldn't let him see the dead-end way she'd felt this morning. "We might go to a city," she said.

"How would you get there?"

"I'm still thinking." She smiled. "What about you?

You live with your parents, I guess?" She hoped the envy she felt didn't show.

"With Mom and Fred. He's my stepdad. It's okay. I like Fred and he's good to me. My own dad works out of the country. South America, Spain, and once even in Iceland. Builds bridges." He sounded wistful.

"So, you don't see him very often?"

"I don't. But it's kind of like I live in two different places."

Jessie screwed up her face.

"One's right here with Mom and Fred." He picked up a stick and drew a box in the sand. "I guess you could say my body lives here." He poked a twig into the sand. "They take care of me. Provide a home and stuff like that." He paused for a moment. "But my real world, the one where the real me lives, is with my dad." To the side of the box he drew a circle. "We talk about important things."

He began setting twigs around the circle.

"See, Dad has a toll-free number that I can call anytime I want. Then he gets the message and calls me in a day or so. He helps me figure my life out. Helps me set goals and then work toward them."

"What kind of goals?"

He shrugged. "For my life. The kind of work I want to do. What classes to take."

"Doesn't you mother care about you, too?"

"Oh, sure. But she doesn't understand me like Dad does. Mom wants me to be a lawyer like Fred. Lawyers make lots of money. And they stay home. Mom never liked Dad being gone all the time." He moved one of the twigs to the center of the circle.

He rearranged himself and lay back on his elbows. Thoughtfully he said, "Dad says you're only a kid about eighteen years, and you might be an adult for sixty or seventy. So a kid's job is to get ready to be an adult. When you have a goal, you measure everything you do as either reaching the goal or not reaching it."

"Hmmm," Jessie murmured. His words struck something deep inside her. "So your goal is to be a news correspondent?"

"That's my long-range goal, sure."

"So what else?"

"Well, getting into the right college, learning to think logically like a newsman has to, lots of things."

He sat up and looked at the tree. "Being able to reach Dad by phone—well, he's like a beacon. He guides me, and he's always there. Caring what happens. The phone links us together. As long as I can reach him, I can take charge of my life. Make it come out the way I want it to."

He smiled before going on. "We both have computers, too, and sometimes I send E-mail. But sometimes I need to hear his voice."

He looked at her and smiled kind of sheepishly, as if he'd just remembered she was there. "I never told anybody all this before," he said.

Such a lump stuck in Jessie's throat that she dared not speak.

"So, to answer your question, I guess maybe I live

in two worlds. One with my body and one with my mind and thoughts." Then he added, "I was supposed to see Dad before school starts, but now maybe he won't be able to get to Los Angeles for a while." Jessie heard the disappointment in his voice.

He jumped to his feet. "Hey, I have to go. But I'll come back." He started off, then turned and said, "Don't worry, I won't tell."

Chapter Fifteen

"Goals."

Jessie sat in the sand halfway down the dune, watching waves break over the ledge. A sliver of moon cast a thin streak of light on the water, and the ocean murmured ominously below. With her arms wrapped around her legs, she rested her head on her knees.

Going back to the house was scary, but they had to eat. And maybe she could get other things they'd need. Especially matches. They could dig clams and scrape black mussels off the rocks if they had a way to cook them. Her thoughts kept turning back to what Jasper had said this morning. How can anybody know what they want for a whole lifetime when they were only kids? Setting goals and working toward them might let normal people take charge of their lives. But not us! How can you set goals when others are always jerking you around, deciding what's best for you?

She flung a stone hard and watched it bounce to the beach below.

Something else he'd said flitted at the back of her thoughts. About keeping in touch with his dad. Jasper said the phone linked them even when his dad was thousands of miles away. She sighed. You had to have someone to link with first. Still, what if she could find her own father?

Dumb thoughts! Where would she ever begin?

The moon had gone down, leaving everything dark, before she ran through the soft sand to the beach and shone her light on the ledge. There'd be precious little time tonight before the tide came rushing back in. When four waves fell short of the ledge, it was time to go.

She crossed the ledge, then ran all the way until she reached the trail. Catching her breath for only a moment, she raced to the top and stood looking toward the house. Something felt different, spooky. "I can't wait," she whispered urgently. "If I don't hurry the tide'll trap me on this side." And she knew there was no place along the beach where she could climb the cliff and force her way through the thickets.

She crossed the field, picking her way around bushes, then crept softly along the board walkway. The pantry door opened silently. She squeezed through and pulled it shut, then hesitated before touching the light switch.

Bright yellow light filled the room, making her blink. Hurry, hurry, she told herself. Still, she felt strange sneaking in like this. But of course Mom and Pop would want them to eat.

She pulled the pack off her back and started toward the shelves. That's when she saw it. Half hidden between the shelves and the freezer was her own pink pack, stuffed full. She opened it and peeked in. Cheese, apples, and other foods, a packet of matches and several flashlight batteries.

Pop had packed it for them! That meant they understood.

As she hoisted the heavy pack to her shoulders, such a feeling of love came over her that she wanted to run upstairs and hug them both. Tears stung her eyes as she turned off the light. For a moment she waited in the darkness, uneasy, then forced herself to open the door.

"So you're back," a man's voice said.

Jessie caught her breath and stood motionless. She squinted, trying to see him. Only blackness filled the space between the buildings.

It wasn't until he went on talking that she realized he was speaking to someone on a portable telephone. He must be around the corner of Pop's tool shed, where a brick path led to the front. The acrid smell of cigarette smoke drifted to her.

"Pretty boring job, watching for kids that'll never show up," the voice went on.

Feeling light-headed, she tiptoed softly, hunkering close to the house in deep shadow. She hesitated at the edge of the field. Goosebumps prickled her arms, and drums seemed to beat in her head.

Stooping low, she moved quickly to the first clump of bushes. Nothing moved. She slid cautiously to the next clump. She wanted to race for the beach. No! Stay calm, she told herself.

At last she reached the dark path and hurried down it. At the bottom of the trail, she realized she'd been holding her breath. She let it out and felt her way to a log, then dropped onto it. Her legs were wobbly, and she was sure she'd never walk again.

Just then a movement in the bushes made her gasp. Jessie yelped as something touched her hand.

A cold nose nuzzled her arm.

"Fielder! You scared me," she whispered. The dog waggled close and put his head on her lap. "What're you doing down here?" She patted his head while he sniffed the backpack, probably smelling the cheese. "Go home, Fielder!" she said. "I don't want you following me." He brushed closer, and by the way his body twisted, she knew he wagged his tail. "Go home! Get!" She dared not yell, and it was hard to make a whisper sound firm. He didn't budge.

I have to go. She could think of something along the way. Maybe he'd get tired of following. She walked south, until she reached the wet sand where her footprints would soon dissolve. But Fielder raced in circles out into the dry sand and back to her. His tracks would give her away for sure. How could she get rid of him?

He ran toward her and raised his big head once more to the backpack.

"You smell the cheese, don't you?" That gave her an idea. If she hid some, dug under some driftwood, made it hard for him to find, maybe that would keep him busy until she could get away. Then, if she walked in the water he wouldn't smell her tracks.

She dropped the pack on the sand and fumbled with

the clasps, not daring to use a light. When she finally got a few slices of cheese out, Fielder was right there, his sopping wet head crowding her.

"Go away!" She dug three holes, all out of reach under chunks of driftwood, and covered the cheese with sand. That would keep him busy for a while.

He was sniffing and digging when she hefted the pack onto her back and took off at a run, the bag whacking her back at each step. Far down the beach she stopped, her breath coming in short gasps and her shoulders aching. If only she dared rest. No, no time for that.

She'd lost Fielder, but she'd wasted precious time and the tide was coming back in. She took off her shoes and slipped a tennie between each strap and her shoulder. The soft uppers formed a cushion and relieved the weight. She ran better barefoot anyway.

When she reached the tide pools, low waves already eddied around the rocks. Even with the flashlight it was hard to pick her way through the maze of fallen boulders. She heaved a sigh when she finally found the passageway and climbed up to it.

Moments later she jumped off the far side of the ledge and dropped her pack. Tiredness and relief pulled her down. The waves rolled up the sandy cove and brushed her bare feet.

Move on, she told herself. She dragged herself to the dune and looked upward. It seemed a mountain. No way could she haul the heavy pack to the top tonight. She dropped in the sand and rested her head in her arms, scrunching her back to take the numbness from her shoulders.

Only the white of the waves gleamed faintly on the dark water. Maybe she'd just stay here until morning. But what if the kids woke up? Went looking for her, even? She stood up and carried the pack back among the rocks, far above the tide line. They'd come down for it in the morning. Nothing would happen to it. She'd never seen any dogs up here, and the seagulls certainly weren't going to fly away with it.

Even so, she felt apprehensive as she climbed the hill, forcing one foot in front of the other with such effort that she wasn't even sure she would make it to the top.

Toady mumbled and flung his arms about when Jessie lay down beside Allie and pulled her jacket around her, wriggling her toes into the cloth of the sleeping bag to get the chill off.

"Where've you been, Jessie?"

Jessie knew from Allie's voice she'd been awake. "I got us some food."

"At the house?"

"Yes."

"Did anyone see you?"

"No." She wouldn't mention the man on the phone.

"How do you know?"

"I'm back." She snuggled into a ball and let the drowsiness tug at her.

"What did you get?"

"Go back to sleep, Allie. You can see in the morning."

"All right." She sounded reluctant.

Was the food really safe down there on the rocks? Nothing there but seagulls.

Warmth folded about her and she gave in to incredible weakness.

Chapter Sixteen

*T*wo seagulls lifted the pink and lavender backpack and flew high into the air. Jessie screamed and raced along the beach after them, "Stop! Come back! You can't have it! We need that food!"

They glided out over the water and dropped it. Each crashing wave buoyed it up, then jostled it seaward.

"Jessie, what's wrong?" Allie's voice cut into her dream.

She opened her eyes and, squinting, tried to focus on the golden fretwork above. As she sat up, she realized it was only the sun shining through the leaves of the tree. The dream had been so real she expected to see the beach and the crashing waves.

"You were hollerin' like everything," Toady said. He stood staring down at her. Both children were fully dressed, so they must have gotten up without Jessie even hearing.

"Just a dream, I guess," she answered, unwinding herself from the sleeping bag.

She looked at her watch. Nine o'clock. "How long you been up?"

Allie shrugged. "Long time. I thought you got some food."

"I did." She jumped to her feet, an urgency drawing her back to the beach.

"Get the other pack and come with me," she ordered. Raising the branches and bursting into blinding sunlight, she ran.

"Wait, Jessie," Allie called.

Jessie's bare feet plowed through the soft sand as she raced downward. Hurry, hurry, hurry! It was that darn dream, but she couldn't feel easy until she knew the food was safe.

Veering left toward the rocks, she strained to catch sight of the pack. She stopped, fear clutching her stomach. A splash of pink lay matted at the edge of the wet sand. Her pack? It couldn't be!

She ran and snatched up the soaked cloth. Empty. "How . . . " she asked, looking around. The tide couldn't have reached the rocks. Could it? No, a wide strip of dry sand lay between here and the spot where she'd left it.

"No, no, no, no," she cried, staring at the rip all down one side. Jessie shook her head, remembering the dream. But gulls couldn't . . .

Bits of cheese and crackers and apples made a trail stretching back to the rocks.

"What's wrong, Jessie?" Allie asked. "What happened?"

Jessie's whole insides felt hollow.

She dropped onto a rock and flung down the bag. She might never get up again, she felt that defeated.

"Jessie! *What's wrong?*" Allie demanded.

Jessie pointed. "See, there? 'Coons. Raccoons got our food." Masses of pointy tracks etched the sand.

Toady picked up a few scattered cans and brought

them to her. Most were without labels, which had washed off in the surf. Or maybe they were ripped off by the 'coons. Three small cans, probably tuna, and two flat sardine cans. The rest must have washed out with the tide. Bits of cheese and cookie crumbs mingled with the loose sand at their feet.

She picked up five half-eaten apples and stared at them. They weren't safe to eat after raccoons or any wild animal had bitten into them. Pop had warned them about that. Reluctantly, she walked to the water's edge and tossed them into the surf.

"Jessie, look!" Toady cried. He'd scrambled up on the rocks and now came back with an unopened box of crackers and several more little cans. "An' there's more apples back there, too."

Jessie took the food and piled it on a flat rock. She opened the crackers and took out one sealed packet.

"Here," she said, picking up a can with a pull tab. "This looks like those little sausages. Open it and eat them with the crackers. Then we'll hunt all over in case there's more scattered on the beach."

She placed the rest of the food in Toady's pack and hefted it. Light as a pillow. Last night the load had cut her shoulder. Dumb. If only she'd taken part of the food up the hill, stashed the cans, and carried the lighter stuff.

While they ate she looked at the pink and lavender pack and remembered the day Mom and Pop had given it to her. Stupid. Fretting over a ruined pack when it's food we need!

"Jessie," Allie said softly, "we'll be all right. At least we got *some* food."

Jessie forced a smile. She couldn't have them feeling as hopeless as she did. Besides, it didn't help to worry about what she should've done.

"Sure we will, Allie." But she was thinking of the one thing they had not found.

After they'd finished eating, Jessie told them. "Hunt everywhere, around rocks and under driftwood. Look for a bright red box of matches, the kind Pop took camping. Even if they got wet they'll still work."

They went over the same places several times, but found only two more cans. The matches probably floated away on the tide, Jessie decided. Little mists rose from the wet sand and drifted around them eerily, until Jessie felt as though she were back in the dream.

She dropped onto a rock and closed her eyes as she listened to the crashing waves now rolling far up the beach, covering anything they might have found.

"Look, Jessie," Toady cried. "It's hermits." The high tide had covered most of the tide pools, but in one small pool at the base of the rock, fish barely an inch long darted and hermit crabs scurried along the bottom.

"How come their shells are all different?" Toady asked.

"I know," Allie said. "We learned it on a field trip. They don't have shells of their own, so they crawl into a shell some other animal has outgrown. When they grow bigger they just find a bigger shell."

"But why don't they have their own shells," Toady demanded as he picked one up and let it walk across his hand, steering it with one finger.

Allie shrugged. "I don't know. Teacher didn't tell us that. Come on, Toady, let's climb that high rock." Carefully he placed the crab back in the water and raced Allie down the beach toward sea stacks that jutted from the sand like eerie giants.

Jessie sat watching the crabs dart here and there. Like us, she thought, always living in somebody else's house.

Maybe it was the muggy heat or her discouragement or because she was still tired, but Jessie's shoulders sagged. Maybe she'd just give up.

Why couldn't Sherrill be a mother? Take care of them like mothers should? She remembered all the times they'd come home from school to find Toady alone and crying, Sherrill passed out on the sofa or sometimes on the floor. Why'd she just think of herself? And why did she drink and do drugs and forget everything else?

"Why'd God give people like that kids?"

She jumped, surprised to find herself shouting, then looked around, hoping Allie and Toady hadn't heard. But they were perched atop the rock far down the beach.

With a sharp stick Jessie gouged lines in the wet sand, the anger still pounding in her head.

What was wrong with Sherrill anyway?

On the way down here from Portland, Mrs. Gates had told them Sherrill had had a rough life. That she couldn't handle responsibility, and that was why she got depressed and drank.

There had been times when she was different. Especially when Wynn, Toady's father, lived with them. Jessie remembered once when Sherill had baked cookies, even. And sometimes she cooked dinner for all of them. But even before Wynn left she'd get up in the morning and sit with a can of beer first thing. And she'd keep drinking all day long.

"Stupid thoughts! Sherrill doesn't care anything about us! Hasn't she said so a hundred times?" She slashed the water again and again with the stick, sending the hermits scurrying beneath rocks.

Spent, she dropped the stick and sat in the sand. Peering into the tide pool, she felt like apologizing to the poor crabs, but they were hiding. Hiding from her. As if she was some ugly monster. Well, she felt like one. An angry monster flailing at something helpless.

Gazing out over the rippling waves calmed her, but she couldn't shake the image of her violent behavior.

"Jessie! Look what Allie found!" Toady's insistent voice shattered her thoughts.

The two children raced toward her, their bare feet slapping the wet sand.

"She found it down there under a pile of drift-wood," he cried, dropping a broken shovel, its handle a short stub, in front of her.

Jessie took it and brushed away dirt and crusted red-brown rust with a stick.

"Looks like there's some solid metal," she said.

Allie's face glowed. "It was under a log, stuck in the sand," she said. "You could even dig clams with it."

"Great," Jessie told them. Now if only they could start a fire. How hungry would they have to be to eat raw clams?

Chapter Seventeen

"We have to start a fire," Jessie said. "And we're going to do it now."

"How?" Toady asked her.

"By rubbing sticks together."

"Hey, good idea," Allie said. "It's easy, I saw it on TV."

"Can I do it?" Toady asked.

"Sure. First, we'll need little pieces of dry driftwood—the smallest you can find. I'll go up and get some paper."

At the tree she dug her book out of the pack, then held it to herself for a moment, hating what she must do. Quickly, she ripped two pages from the front. At least they weren't story pages.

When she reached the beach again, Toady and Allie had gathered tiny pieces of dried seaweed and wood into a pile. Jessie found a smooth stick and a board.

"How long will it take?" Toady asked.

Jessie placed the tip of the stick on the board and rubbed her hands rapidly back and forth, twirling the stick. "See, it gets hot, and that will light the paper."

But the stick flew out of her hand. She picked it up and started again. The only stick they found had edges and she couldn't get it to stay in one place on the board.

"Hold the paper close," she told Toady.

Before long her hands felt sore and she discovered a blister.

"Let me try, I know how." Toady teased.

"Go ahead," Jessie told him, wondering what they were doing wrong.

After several tries, Toady threw the stick down and cried, "It don't work!"

"We must not be doing it right," Jessie told him. She put the stick aside and gathered up what food was left. Picking up her pink pack and brushing off the sand, she trudged back up the hill.

At the tree Jessie took stock of their food. If they were careful—if they ate only two meals each day—they'd have enough for today and tomorrow.

"I'm hungry," Toady said.

"It's way past lunchtime," Jessie told him. "I'll open two cans and we'll finish the bananas."

"Good! I'm starving."

"Me too," Allie added.

Starving. She remembered times in Portland when hunger had made her stomach feel pulled in, like a balloon with all the air leaked out. And just when it had seemed they could stand it no longer, a neighbor would bring them leftovers from her own dinner, or they'd find something where restaurants threw stuff out, or the social worker would come. But there were no neighbors or restaurants here and the only social worker . . . She couldn't finish the thought for the blurry feeling inside her head. Would they starve?

It would be days before the tide was low enough to go back. Go back? No! That would be giving up, failing.

Beneath the tree the air felt muggy, and she pushed back her hair. It would be cool in the top of the tree. She glanced up, remembering the days she'd sat lost in other worlds, wishing she could climb up there now and forget everything. No, that would be giving up, too!

She opened two cans, both tuna fish, and set them on a T-shirt. The smell made her mouth fill with saliva and her stomach twist into a knot.

They sat on the ground around the meager meal.

I ought to say a blessing like Pop always does, Jessie thought. Toady and Allie waited as if they expected it as well.

"Dear God," she began, feeling self-conscious, but trying not to show it. Why couldn't she think of one of the prayers they'd learned in Sunday school? Still, those didn't seem right for now either. "Thank you for this food. And thank you for this tree. And for helping us. Amen."

"That was a good prayer, Jessie," Allie said softly.

They ate in silence, as though savoring each bite took concentration. Then Allie and Toady drank the liquid from the cans.

Jessie again checked their food, trying to figure a way to make it last longer. Maybe they could find some blackberries: they were ripe now. Besides, she'd read that you wouldn't starve if you didn't eat for a day or two. As long as you had water.

Toady stood watching her. "I can go back and get my fishing pole and catch some fish," Toady said.

"No!" Jessie cried, then said more softly, "No, Toady."

"Why not? You went back."

"It's too risky." She told them about the man. "None of us can go back."

"Ever?" Toady asked.

"Not for now."

"But *how'll* we know when we can go back?" Allie demanded.

Jessie shook her head. "I still don't know."

"What'll we do when school starts?" Toady asked. "I'll be in second grade."

Jessie sighed. "That's weeks yet, Toady, so don't worry about it." Wasn't it enough to try to figure out what they'd eat tomorrow and the next day and the day after?

"Can I climb up to the crow's nest?" Toady begged.

"Sure. Keep a sharp look out, Matey."

"Jessie!" Toady cried from the treetop, "they're comin'."

"Pirates?" Jessie asked.

"No. Two men," he said in a loud whisper. "They just drove through the gate above the house. In a white pickup. They're lookin' around."

Jessie jumped to her feet. "You sure, Toady?"

"They . . ."

"Come down quick!" Jessie cried, scooping everything into their packs.

"They're starting down the trail," Toady called.

"Get down here!"

Toady dropped to the ground.

"We have to hide," Jessie said, loaded down with their stuff. "But *where?*" Why hadn't she planned for this?

"How about the maze?" Allie asked.

When Jessie looked puzzled, she added, "Where the deer sleep."

Jessie hesitated but a moment. "Yeah," she said. Gathering their things, she parceled them out to Toady and Allie, then stooped beneath the low branches.

They crept outside, hunkering down close to the wall of salal until they reached the animal path. Silently they filed along the deer's narrow trail to the circle of grass. Prickles of fear ran along Jessie's spine.

"Now, keep quiet," she whispered. She dropped her load in a heap. A strong, musky animal odor filled the air. Had they gotten everything this time? At least they didn't have clothes hanging in the tree.

Allie gasped at voices close by. "Will they find us?" she whispered.

"Shhh."

"I told them this was crazy," a man's voice said. "Kids couldn't climb that fence. Besides, it's eight or nine miles out here by road."

"Well, you never know," another voice said. "And it's not that far by the beach. Maybe a couple of miles."

"Huh!" The first man snorted. "Look down there. No way. Solid rock juts into the water at both ends of Bjorset Cove. And that brush between here and the Harmon farm is so thick a weasel couldn't get through."

"Hey, looks like something's been under this tree."

Allie clutched Jessie's arm in alarm.

"Deer, more'n likely. Come on, we'll tramp that field and then get back up the hill. We won't find them here."

The voices grew fainter as the men moved away, but Jessie, feeling clammy all over, sat with a child on each side of her. No one spoke for a long time.

After an hour Jessie dug into one of the bags and took out a can with a pull tab. She opened it and divided the little sausages among them.

"When can we go back to the tree?" Toady whispered.

"Soon, I guess," Jessie told him. She had a spooky feeling about leaving their hideout, even though she was sure the men were gone.

When they'd finished eating, Jessie cautiously led the way back to the tree. At once Toady scrambled to the top and called out softly, "All's clear."

Jessie smiled. Good thing he'd climbed up there this morning. Otherwise . . .

"Let's leave everything in the packs," she told Allie.

"I'm still hungry," Toady called from his perch.

"We'll clean out the peanut butter jar," she said.

Toady came down the tree and hung upside down

while he licked the plastic spoon Jessie handed him.

"Look," Jessie said, "we have to find something more to eat."

Toady slithered out onto the limb and hung just above her head, handing the spoon back for a refill.

"Do you think you could eat raw clams?" Jessie asked.

"Yuck!" Toady said.

Allie made a barfing noise.

"Well then, we have to start a fire somehow."

That evening, after she'd tucked the children into bed, Jessie went out and sat at the top of the dune. Moonlight painted a wide swath of yellow across the water. Rocks rose like black pillars, and the waves that broke against them shattered into cold, white beads.

Where had those thoughts come from this morning? About Sherrill? The anger didn't eat her up now, but was it true? Maybe Sherrill couldn't do anything but give up. Maybe she didn't know how to stay strong.

I won't give up! I'll never give up! Jessie told herself. She'd think of something. That boy, Jasper, would come back. Maybe he could get a message to Mom and Pop without the spies knowing.

Another thought needled her. She relived her awful anger. Remembered how she'd whacked the stick across the tide pool. Over and over. Could she beat someone? In anger? Was that the way it happened for Sherrill? Was she like Sherrill?

Chapter Eighteen

 hree days. They'd been here three days, and today was the fourth. Jessie scratched a line beside the date on the tide book. She kept going over their food supply, switching things around, trying to think of ways to make it last longer. They'd finished the crackers and most of the cans of tuna and sardines.

Jasper hadn't returned as he'd promised. Maybe he wasn't coming back at all. Probably too busy to be bothered with kids.

"Jessie, are we going to starve?" Allie asked.

"Of course not," Jessie said, wondering if she really believed it.

"I can catch a fish. A big one! Maybe a salmon!" Toady boasted.

Laughing, Jessie rumpled his blond hair. "With what?" she asked.

"Oh, yeah. Well, why didn't we bring any fishing stuff?"

"Same reason we didn't bring lots of things," Jessie told him. "But blackberries are ripe. We'll pick some after a bit, and that will stretch our other stuff, make it last longer."

"I'm still hungry," Toady complained.

"Well, there's still a little peanut butter around the edges of the jar." Jessie handed it to him.

Toady and Allie went out to the sand behind the tree to play. Jessie stood for several moments looking up at the perch. How she'd like to climb up there now, settle in and read and pretend everything was right. Pretend that her only concern was to get back across the rocks before the tide came in. To get home on time.

Home. She sighed as she went into the hot sun and breathed in the smell of dry grass and the heady incense of blooming brush. Those very smells had greeted her when Mrs. Gates first brought them to live with Mom and Pop two years ago. "The only place we ever thought of as home," she said aloud. "That ought to count for something." Another thought seemed to nudge at her consciousness, but it wouldn't surface. "Home." The word seemed to hang there in the air. "But what does it mean?" Forget it, she told herself, impatience crowding her mind. We don't have a home.

She remembered Mrs. Gates saying, "I hope you will be here for a long time."

"And never go back to Sherrill?" Jessie had asked.

That's when Mrs. Gates said such a peculiar thing. "Don't judge her too harshly, Jessie. I suspect your mother had a difficult childhood, and she's never gotten over it."

"But she's a grown-up now," Jessie had objected.

Mrs. Gates had smiled at her. "We don't outgrow some things, Jessie. We have to work through them. What happens to children often lives with them forever. Perhaps your mother would like to be different. Perhaps she doesn't know how."

Had she ever been different? Jessie wondered.

Jessie closed her eyes. She was sitting beside a pair of men's boots, boots with nails in the bottom, and she felt safe, and someone spoke her name, softly, lovingly. "Jessie."

It was a picture she'd seen in her mind many times, but she'd never told anyone. Was it real or only part of her imagination? Or something she'd read in a book? And if it was real, who belonged to the boots? Boots with nails in the bottom. Who ever heard of such a thing? But, as always, the other question followed. Did the boots belong to her father?

Her eyes flew open. The whole matter seemed silly now, standing here in the field, with her eyes open, with the sun shining hot. Except, today, she kept on thinking about that voice—the one that said "Jessie" in a way no one had ever spoken her name. She made a face, wishing she could blot out those thoughts. Her very name was another puzzle. A real name. She remembered how Sherrill used to laugh and say to her friends, "Allie? She's just an old alley cat." And Jessie remembered the first time she had seen Toady, all red and bald and wrinkled. "Looks like a toad," Sherrill had said. "Good name, Toad." And so she'd named him Toady.

But she, Jessie, had a real name. Jessica. Sherrill never said anything about her name. Mom called it a good old-fashioned name.

Toady came and joined her. "I'm thirsty," he complained.

"Well, go get some water."

She'd just gone back under the tree when she heard Toady yelling.

Frantic, she flew out the back door and along the path, with Allie close behind.

Halfway to the faucet they spotted Toady. He was tugging at what looked like a dark red box.

"What is it?" Jessie called, relieved not to find someone trying to drag him away.

"An ice chest," he said, when they reached his side. "It was stuffed way back in that big box by the faucet. An' look." He threw the lid open, and Jessie gasped.

Inside were oranges, a large bag of peanuts, chocolate bars, a bag of mixed dried fruit, and lots of little packages of cheese. Jessie took a deep breath, savoring the mingled smells.

"Toady, where'd it come from?"

"I dunno. Somebody hid it there."

"It might be a trap." What if those two men who were here yesterday hid it and were watching now? Jessie raised her head and looked all about, up the hill toward the house, out over the ocean.

"Can we eat?" Toady asked.

Jessie signaled them to be quiet and stood listening. No sound came except the ocean below. If it was a trap, they were already caught.

"Was there a note or anything with it?"

"Nope. Just the chest. Shoved way back in that box."

"After this, Toady," she told him, "you climb the tree and make sure all's clear before anybody goes up to the faucet." She picked up the chest and headed toward the tree.

"He didn't get any water," Allie said.

" 'Course not, I couldn't carry it."

"Never mind, we'll each eat an orange," Jessie soothed them.

When they reached the tree, she set out three oranges and a package of cheese. They'd eat that for lunch, then each have a chocolate bar for dessert. Her mouth watered as she lifted the candy out.

"It's almost melted," she said. "I guess we'll have to lick it off the paper. And the ice packs are thawed, so it must have been there since morning. Good thing those men didn't see it."

"It was way back in that box," Toady told her.

Jessie opened the bag of peanuts and poured out three piles. "Nuts are good for us," she said.

"Toady should say the blessing," Allie told her.

They bowed their heads while Toady prayed the same prayer he always said at bedtime, with all the "blesses" for each member of the family. Finally he said, "Thank you for whoever left the food. Amen." He opened his eyes and started to peel an orange.

"I think Jasper left that chest," Allie said.

Toady nodded. "I bet he did, too."

"But why would he leave it there? Why not bring it on down? He said he'd come back and he hasn't."

"He had a reason," Toady said as he stuffed a section of orange into his mouth.

When they'd finished eating, Allie and Toady raced about, laughing and playing, probably because the food they'd eaten gave them new energy. Jessie packed the rest of the food away in a backpack.

"Can we have some more peanuts?" Toady begged. Jessie started to say they had to save them. But it was so tempting that she poured each of them another handful and took some herself. They'd eat the last of the sardines tonight. Oranges in the morning, some of the other fruit for lunch. That left only peanuts and the cheese for tomorrow night. She sighed. It had seemed like so much food, but it, too, would soon be gone.

"I'm going up to the faucet," Jessie told Allie.

"Wait'll I check," Toady said, already scrambling up the tree. Soon he gave an all clear.

When she reached the faucet she bent down and drank deeply, then took the margarine tub Toady had dropped and filled it.

She hunted all about but found no note.

Allie was right. It had to be Jasper. He must have had to go somewhere and left it early this morning.

She returned to the tree and found Toady playing in the sand. Our patio. She grinned at the thought.

When she raised a branch and stepped beneath the tree, Toady picked up his stickmen and followed.

"Allie, what on earth?"

Allie sat propped against the tree. On one side of

her was a pile of chinquapin burrs. The bottom of one of the plastic tubs was covered with nuts. Her fingers looked red and sore from the burrs.

"I'm shelling nuts for us to eat," she said.

"How'd you get them?" Jessie asked, looking up, remembering Allie's fear of climbing. "Did you climb the tree?"

"A ways," Allie said.

Jessie sat down and picked up a large chinquapin burr. Gently she parted the stickery cup that held the nut.

"Ouch!" she said as the needles jabbed her fingers. She sucked on it to stop the stinging. How had Allie managed to shell out so many?

"I'll crack them," Toady said.

They worked in silence for some time. But Allie shelled out three nuts to Jessie's one.

"You're good at this," Jessie said.

"I'm glad I'm good at something," Allie said.

"Allie! You're good at lots of things."

"No, I'm not. Mom always has you do the important jobs because I can't."

"That's not it, Allie. Mom doesn't want you to overdo and get sick, that's all."

Allie shrugged. "Same thing."

Jessie stared at her sister.

"Allie, you untie knots better'n anybody," Toady said.

Allie looked up and smiled. "Yeah," she said, "I guess that's two things I do good."

"An' you found the shovel."

Allie grinned.

They gathered the prickly hulls and carried them outside. Jessie stood for several moments looking out across the water. Streaks of deep purple painted the sky, and a faint pink glow marked the horizon. We'll make it, she told herself. We won't give up.

Chapter Nineteen

*N*o food. For two days they'd had only nuts and berries. How long could they live like that, Jessie wondered. She stared at the tide book, wondering if this was the sixth or seventh day. Some days she couldn't remember if she'd marked their calendar or not.

Each morning Toady went up to the faucet hoping to find another ice chest and moped when he came back empty-handed. He kept a vigil in the crow's nest but saw no one. And Jasper had not returned.

The idea of eating raw clams or mussels still turned Jessie's stomach. Maybe we aren't hungry enough yet, she decided.

Late one afternoon, after she and Allie had cracked nuts for over an hour, they carried the hulls outside. They had started back for the tree, when Allie suddenly stopped.

"Jessie, look!" she cried. She pointed to the south.

Beyond the cliff, a long bluish curl spiraled upward, then thinned to gray as the breeze carried it over the ocean. Smoke!

"It's a *fire!*" Toady exclaimed.

"Maybe it's somebody picnicking," Allie danced up and down with excitement. "Maybe they'll leave it burning. Maybe we could go cook clams on it. Or maybe we could ask . . . "

"It's around the point," Jessie said. "Why would anybody walk that far? It's better'n three miles from the state park," she mused aloud.

"Let's go over and see," Toady said.

"We'll have to wait for low tide," Jessie answered without taking her eyes off the thin gray line against the sky. It might be somebody looking for us. The thought sent a shiver along her spine. "No, I'd better go alone. Later," she added.

"But Allie saw it," Toady protested.

Jessie smiled at him. "I know. But someone might see us. And three of us might remind them of three missing children. Okay?"

"I guess."

"We'll stay here, Jessie," Allie said soberly.

Jessie ducked beneath the tree and dug in her jacket pocket for the tide book. Low tide wasn't until 3:30 in the morning, and it wasn't a very low tide at all. If she had the right day . . . She sighed, wishing she'd kept better track, had marked the day first thing when she woke up.

At least it'd still be dark. And probably if it was picnickers they'd be gone. But would there still be coals burning? Or would they pour on water to make sure it was clean out?

"I could climb over that cliff," Toady said.

"It's too dangerous, Toady. The rocks are crumbly. If you fell . . . "

"I know," he said.

"We'll eat our berries and nuts now, then we'll go

to the beach and wait." She didn't add that she needed to watch the waves in case her calculations were wrong. "We'll need dry wood to get a fire going. If I can get some coals."

"What's the shovel for?" Toady asked on the way to the beach.

"I read once about a pioneer girl carrying coals with a shovel. To start a fire when theirs had gone out."

"Didn't she have any matches either?" Toady asked.

"They didn't have matches then, I guess."

The tide line had hardly changed from this afternoon's high.

"I can't see the smoke now," Toady said. "Did it go out?"

"Probably because it's dark," Jessie told him.

"If we build a fire out in the open someone might see it," she added. "But behind one of those big rocks it would be hidden. Especially if we keep it small."

"How'll we keep it burning at night?" Toady asked.

"Same way we did in the mountains. Remember?"

"Oh, yeah. Pop dug a hole and put on a big chunk of wood."

"He called it banking," Allie said.

"I know," Toady replied. "Think I'd forget?"

"Hey, no arguing," Jessie told them. She had stopped where several sea stacks, enormous rock formations that jutted high into the air, formed a barrier between them and the ocean. "This is a good spot," she said. "The rocks block the wind, and no one can see us." She picked up several beach rocks and placed them in a small ring in the sand. "We'll cook here," she said.

"Yeah!" Toady exclaimed. "Want us to find some wood?"

"Sure, but gather some of that tiny stuff with the dried-up seaweed in it to get it burning."

Jessie dug in her pocket for the pages she'd torn from her book and crumpled them in the center of the ring of stones. Toady and Allie piled on bits of beach drift and stacked chunks of driftwood to one side.

"Jessie, the light's so weak I can't see," Toady complained. The flashlight held the last of their batteries.

A thin crescent of moon had risen and now cast a pale glow over everything.

"Hold the light on my watch," Jessie said. "Better go now, it's close to low." She'd watched the white splash of waves reflected in the moonlight.

"We'll find more wood," Allie said.

Jessie took off her shoes and crossed the ledge quickly, with water sucking at the base of the rock and sloshing over her bare feet.

Before she dropped to the tide pools, she saw the red glare far down the beach and felt like shouting for joy. Instead, she sprinted along the wet sand until she came close. As she turned toward the bluff and the fire, soft, warm sand caressed her feet. The smell of smoke, mingled with the savory odor of cooked meat, wafted toward her.

She was almost at the fire when something moved

at the far side. Two dark humps in the sand. People. In sleeping bags.

She moved slowly, watching the humps. One of them turned and an arm was flung into the air. Holding her breath, Jessie waited, her heart pounding. The second hump mumbled and rolled over, then all was quiet. So quiet the ocean seemed to roar. Or was it her head?

Once more she moved forward, a step at a time, until she felt the warmth of the fire. She slid the shovel under red coals. The fire snapped, making her jump. She waited, crouched low, her eyes on the sleeping bags. No movement.

Heat from the fire seared her arms and face. Careful, she told herself as she pulled the shovel back from the fire.

Now back up, she told herself. One step. Another. She scuffed her feet through the sand to cover her tracks. Neither hump moved.

Finally, far enough away to feel safe, she set the shovel down in the sand. Her arms burned from the heat. She wanted to run to the surf and dip them into the salty water, but that would waste time and the coals might go out before she got back. A jacket would have protected her arms, but who would think of one on such a warm night? She decided to stay in the dry sand and not chance a sneaker wave putting out the fire.

When she reached the tide pools she set the shovel down and soaked her arms in the cool water before starting across.

She needed both hands to hold the shovel, so she steadied herself by leaning her shoulder against the cliff, grateful for the thin moonlight. Taking tiny sideways steps, she hardly dared breathe. At last she reached the far side and dropped to the beach.

Some of the coals had turned black, but underneath they still glowed red.

Carrying them to the fire ring, Jessie dumped them on the paper and kindling. The paper caught and flared up. Slowly, yellow flame nibbled at the wood, and wisps of smoke curled away.

"I did it!" she shouted. "I got us fire! Allie! Toady! Where are you?"

She laid two pieces of wood on the fire. Soon the flames sparked red and blue, and smoke rose, stinging her eyes.

"You got it!" Allie yelled, as both children came around one of the rocks.

"Look, Jessie!" Toady cried. He stopped in front of her and held out a tin can with several black mussels in it. "We scraped them off the rocks with the knife."

"Can we cook them?" Allie asked.

"Why not?" Jessie hardly trusted the feelings that welled up inside her, and tears stung her eyes.

"First let's get a fire going under a stump. That way it can burn all the time, and we can scoop out coals for cooking." The stump she chose was well back from the tide line, and far enough from the piles of driftwood to be safe. She scooped sand from below the stump, then laid pieces of dry driftwood at the bottom. She used the shovel to transfer some of the burning wood to the hole. It smoldered for a while but soon caught and began to burn.

"We'll bank it with larger pieces the way Pop showed us," she told Allie and Toady. "Now, let's cook those mussels."

"We didn't have any fire, and now we have two," Toady sang, as he raced in circles, dragging a long rope of kelp and snapping it like a whip.

When the fire in the ring had burned down to coals, Jessie piled on a mass of wet kelp and buried the mussels in the hissing, odorous tangle.

"How'll we get them off the fire?" Allie asked.

When the shells popped open, Jessie found two driftwood sticks and lifted each shell onto a flat chunk of driftwood. Orange-colored meat bulged from each shell.

"They're hot," she warned.

As soon as the mussels had cooled, they all dug the chewy meat from the shells with their fingers and poked it into their mouths.

"That tasted better'n anything I ever ate," Allie said.

"Yeah," Toady agreed, licking the inside of a shell for the last drop of juice.

"Was it hard? Getting the coals?" Allie asked.

Jessie told about the people sleeping nearby and how scared she had been.

The wood beneath the stump had burned low, so Jessie found two huge, knotty chunks and placed them on the smaller wood in the hole.

"There, that should burn all night."

"Can we sleep here? By the fire?" Allie asked.

"Sure, why not?" It wasn't cold. If they went back to the tree, she'd worry about the fire going out. Here, she could keep an eye on it. Besides, the sky was already showing morning light. Before the tide came all the way in she'd try to dig some clams.

"I like camping here," Toady said. "We could live here forever."

"Sure," Jessie said. She wouldn't douse Toady's enthusiasm, not tonight.

Allie and Toady curled up in the warm sand next to a large rock, pulled their coats over themselves, and were soon asleep. The cooking fire had died down quickly. No one out in a boat could see them here behind the rocks anyway, Jessie decided, as she climbed onto one of the stacks to peer out over the ocean.

She sat in the darkness after the moon had set in the west. Only the swish-swishing of waves and the occasional crackling of the fire below broke the stillness. Far out on the ocean, streaks of light shone from beneath the water, the phosphorescence that Pop said was caused by some kind of algae. She'd only seen it once before. Maybe it was a good sign.

Pop. How she longed for Mom and Pop. Suddenly she sat up, her mind whirling. *We never missed any of the other people when we left!* Her question of the other day seemed to burn in her mind. *What's a home?* Sure, the other places were nice to stay in, some of them.

But different. Maybe those other people didn't miss us either! People who loved you—people you could count on. Something kept on going even when you were apart! Somehow, that was important, though Jessie wasn't sure why it made any difference now. She was too exhausted to think clearly. She found her way back to the sand, propped herself against a rock, pulled her jacket about her, and drifted into sleep.

Chapter Twenty

"*J*essiee! Jessiee! Jessiee!"

It seemed she'd hardly slept when someone called her name, over and over.

She opened her eyes and stared upward. Empty sky. Scarcely daylight. It took a moment to remember why she was on the beach. She sat up quickly.

"Jessie! Jessie! Come and see!"

Toady.

Still confused, she got up and found her way around the tall rocks. Far down the beach Toady ran, hitching along as though dragging something.

"Look what I found!" he yelled as Jessie came closer.

"I can fish!" Toady cried even before she reached him.

At his feet lay a huge tangled heap of kelp, the bulky tubes and rubbery leaves entwined with silvery fish line and brilliant pink and orange beads. One piece of line was attached to a hook.

"Somebody lost their fishing stuff and it washed up on the beach," Toady explained.

"You'll have to untangle it first," Jessie told him. She knelt and tried to wrench the bulbous kelp apart with her hands. "We'll need the knife," she said when the long, wet coils refused to give.

She grabbed a length of the seaweed and helped drag it through the sand and around near the fire. Allie was awake and squatted there, placing driftwood on the smoldering coals.

"What is it?" she asked.

"Fishin' line," Toady boasted. "Only it's all tangled." He reached down and began yanking at the line.

"Don't," Jessie said. "You'll just make it harder to untangle."

"Well, how'll I get it?" he demanded.

"You'll have to cut the kelp and untangle it," Jessie said.

"I can't," he said stubbornly. "It's a mess."

Jessie stood silent. Looking at the smelly pile, she felt the same frustration. It'd take forever.

"Right now I've got to dig for some clams or find some mussels. Tide's still kind of low." She picked up the stubby shovel and the can Toady had found. "Wait 'til I get back," she told them, and ran down the beach.

The surf was a thin line of white foam, but only a few rocks remained uncovered. Still, lots of times you could find butter clams close to shore. Or maybe a cluster of black mussels on the rocks.

She waded into the tide pools, picking her way around the pretty green and pink sea anemones that clung to the bottom and looked like big fluffy flowers. Stopping beside a rock higher than her head, she began digging at its base. The strong clammy smell made her hurry. She scratched and dug in the gravel, until she'd found several clams. Hot sun beat down on her back before the rush of waves forced her to stop digging. "But today we'll eat," she said aloud.

Even before she reached their camp she saw Allie and Toady bent over the clump of seaweed. Strewn on the hot sand lay skinny brown logs of kelp. Long strings of fishing line lay fanned out on a piece of driftwood.

"Lookit, Jessie," Toady shouted. "Allie got it untangled. An' there's *three* hooks!"

Allie ran and took the can of clams from Jessie's hand.

"Wow! You got lots," she said.

"We could tie the line onto a stick," Jessie said.

Grinning, Toady picked up a slender white limb. "I found it while Allie was gettin' the line untangled."

Jessie tested the pole and decided it would hold small fish. She used the knife to notch around the tip, then started to tie on a piece of fish line.

"Wait," Toady said, taking the stick from her. "Pop showed me how to tie it." He changed the knot, then knotted a hook on the other end.

"He can use one of the little clams for bait," Allie said.

"If a whale takes it he might pull me clear to the middle of the ocean!"

They all laughed.

"I'll sit on a rock," Toady said, his eyes bright with excitement. "Pop says fish feed around the rocks."

They walked out to the open beach, and Jessie surveyed the rocks jutting into the water.

"That big flat one should be good, Toady."

He ran and climbed onto it and picked his way to the far side, then peered down to the deep water.

"Be careful," Jessie called. "And remember, the tide's coming in."

She kept an anxious eye on the little boy. He so wanted to feel grown up, she reminded herself.

In moments she heard a shriek from the rock and, heart pounding, raced around to see what was wrong. Toady waved a small fish.

"Come and get it," he called. "I don't have anything to put it in."

Jessie waded through the waves and climbed up to take the fish. Before the tide covered the beach side of the rock Toady had caught six perch.

"Boy, we're gonna eat today!" he said as he helped Jessie cut off the heads and scrape out the insides. "We'll save the heads for bait," Toady added.

Allie had a fire going in the ring of rocks when they returned, and Jessie piled on a clump of seaweed and placed the fish on top.

"They'll steam that way," she said.

When the fish were done, the children picked the meat from the bones and stuffed it into their mouths. They'd save the clams for tonight, Jessie thought.

"Jessie, we could stay here forever, couldn't we?" Toady said.

Forever, Jessie thought. How long was forever?

Chapter Twenty-One

*J*essie parted branches damp with dew.

"Oh, no!" she cried. Thick gray fog shrouded the hillside and touched her face with dampness.

At the the cliff she found the beach obscured by mist, the air strong with the smell of seaweed and fish. Good thing they'd returned to the tree last night.

Soon she'd have to dig clams for breakfast. If only she knew what day it was, then she'd know for sure when the tide was lowest, when it would start back in. How many times had she missed marking the days?

Clams again! Last night they'd choked down each bite, trying to pretend it was steak or hamburger. She could hardly believe how good they'd tasted only a few days ago.

"I'd rather eat seaweed," Toady said, and Jessie almost agreed.

She hurried down the dune and poked chunks of wood beneath the stump. Soon the fire blazed.

She surveyed the neat pile of wood Toady had gathered without anyone telling him. He'd even sorted it, one pile for daytime and large, knotty chunks to bank the fire at night.

She peered through the gray fog. "Doesn't look like the kind that burns off," she told a hovering seagull. Fog like that could hang on for days. Cold and wet, soaking everything. *And bringing on Allie's asthma.*

"Jessie," Toady squealed as he came up behind her, "you got a good enough fire for roastin' hot dogs."

Jessie grinned. "Sure do, *if* we had some hot dogs. You did a good job gathering wood."

"It keeps us warm," he said, wrapping his arms around Jessie's waist and hugging her.

"You cold?"

He shivered and nodded his head.

"Where's Allie?"

"Still in bed."

"Is she okay?"

Toady shrugged. "I guess."

Better go and see, Jessie decided. She tossed two more chunks of wood on the fire. "I'll be right back."

Allie sat up, the sleeping bag wrapped around herself.

"Allie. You all right?"

She sighed heavily. "I'm tired." She shivered and pulled the bag closer. "I think I'll stay in bed awhile."

"Well . . . ." Jessie hesitated. "Look, Allie, I've got to dig clams. Then I'll be back. You rest. There's a good fire on the beach if you feel like going down there."

Allie pulled the bag over her head.

"I'm hungry," Toady said, coming through their back door.

"Allie's tired," Jessie said. "Let her sleep," She grabbed the broken shovel. "I want you to stay here until I come back. Pick some nuts to eat."

"Awww," the boy said. He held his fish line. "I was gonna fish."

"You can do that when the tide's high. I have to dig while it's low."

"Clams again? Yuck!" Toady made a face. He'd caught no fish the past two days.

He followed her outside. When they were a way from the tree, Jesse turned and told him. "I'm worried about Allie. You stay there. If she starts coughing or wheezing you come and get me. Understand?"

"I don't want to stay here."

"You'll have to. As soon as I get back you can fish."

"She's just lazy. I'm goin' fishin'. Besides, I don't want any more old clams."

"Toady!" She said it sternly.

"Oh, all right." He stomped back to the tree, and Jessie went to the beach.

Maybe it was worrying about Allie, or maybe there just weren't any clams, but Jessie had dug only seven by the time little waves began nibbling at her holes. Funny how one minute the tide was still going out, so quiet you weren't even aware, and the next everything changed. First, a low rustling among the eel grass and kelp. Then the first swell of water, slithering around rocks, seeping beneath her shoes, and the low rumble of the ocean as though it came from far away.

Mist blotted out the shoreline, and Jessie couldn't tell how far she'd come. Maybe farther than she should have. Rocks crusted with orange and purple starfish surrounded her, and patches of eel grass waved ominously in the surf.

Waves pounded, and an insistent growl came from the deep. Terns cried their shrill cries, then grew silent. A wave broke over her ankles, making her hurry faster.

Fog formed a gray wall, hiding even the beach, showing only dim shapes of nearby rocks.

She moved shoreward until at a patch of gravel she caught the strong smell of clams.

"Must be a bunch in here," she said aloud. If she hurried . . .

Before she bent to dig she glanced up. For a brief moment the mists swirled and she saw Toady standing at the top of the dune, waving his arms wildly.

"I'm coming," she yelled although she knew the ocean drowned her words. She grabbed the shovel and the can of clams. The water rushed behind her. If Allie was really bad . . .

"I shouldn't have left her." She remembered times when Mom stayed up all night, times when Allie fought for every breath.

Picking her way through and around tide pools was too slow. She tried what seemed like a short-cut between the rocks, leaping from one to the next, hurling herself across a sand spit and onto another rock, balancing so she wouldn't drop the can and the shovel. Once she slipped and scraped her knee on rough barnacles.

She waded through a tide pool, the salty water stinging her knee, and stumbled across smaller rocks.

Which way should she go? Nothing looked familiar, and she couldn't see the beach. Could a person go in circles out here? Get lost like in the woods? She felt panic rising inside.

A wave crashed behind her.

Keep the waves in back, she told herself.

The rocks were smaller now. Maybe this was the way she'd come. She jumped from one to another, each time reeling on slippery sea lettuce that covered everything.

As she leaped for the next rock, her foot touched, then slipped. She felt herself falling, the water below coming at her, then the jarring crash as she landed.

For a moment she lay stunned, the ocean foaming around her. She raised her wet arms. They worked all right. She tried to stand, but searing pain shot through her left ankle. With difficulty she managed to get up and stand on her right leg.

"The clams!" she cried. "And the shovel." She must not lose them. But how was she to hobble through tide pools and over rocks?

She found the clams scattered among green and pink sea anemones and plopped them back into the can. But the shovel lay behind her, and was now covered by water. Only a few steps. Did she dare go back? A wave almost knocked her down.

"I have to get to the beach," she cried, hopping forward on her good leg.

When she looked up the fog swirled once more, and for a moment she could make out the cliff and the tree. At least she was headed in the right direction!

Balancing on one foot, she braced against rocks to steady her steps and with each step set the can of clams as far ahead as she could reach. In some places there were no rocks tall enough to steady her, and limping through tide pools was slow. She gritted her teeth at the sharp pain in her ankle.

"It's not broken," she told herself, "or I wouldn't be able to move it."

The ominous roar of inrushing waves brought on a feeling of panic.

Rocks blocked her way. She moved sideways, clutching them, grabbing onto slimy seaweed. Resting a moment, she lowered her swollen ankle in the icy water.

Slap! Waves slammed the rocks. She dared not look back. Pulling herself onto the lowest rock, she swung her legs to the other side. Splinters of pain ricocheted through her whole body. She lay against the rock for a moment, until spray spewed over her, sending ripples of fear along her spine. Hurry, hurry! She balanced on the good foot and threw herself toward the next rock. Water swirled around her knees. She barely clung to the rock as the wave sucked back out. The tide was sweeping in faster than she could move!

Chapter Twenty-Two

Suddenly she heard her name ring out in the fog. Moments later, Allie and Toady splashed through the water.

"What happened?" Allie asked.

"I fell."

"See? I told you," Toady cried.

Allie took the can of clams and handed it to Toady.

"Take these to the beach," she ordered. "Now, lean on me," Allie told Jessie. "We have to hurry. The tide's coming in."

"You can't hold me . . . " Jessie began.

"Do it."

Jessie stared at her sister, then steadied herself against Allie's shoulder as she hopped on her good foot. When they came to rocks, Allie helped her over. Waves splashed them both, but they moved forward, while Jessie gritted her teeth against the pain.

They reached the beach at last and collapsed onto the sand, dripping wet and out of breath.

"We made it!" Jessie said.

Allie grinned. "I knew we would."

"But I lost the shovel."

"It's okay. You're safe," Allie said.

They sat watching waves sweep in, covering the rocks where they had stood only moments before.

"Thanks, Allie," Jessie said. "For a while I thought those waves had me for sure."

Then she remembered. "I thought you were sick. I thought your asthma . . . "

"I wasn't sick," Allie said. "I was scared I'd get sick. I thought if I got clear down in the sleeping bag the fog couldn't get me."

"Why'd Toady call me then?"

Toady looked sheepish. "I wanted to go fishing. I didn't mean to make you fall."

"But how'd you know?"

"I saw you. The fog was swirlin', and part of the time I could see you out there. I saw you fall and hollered at Allie."

"Your ankle's really swollen," Allie said. "Let's get you up to the fire. "

"If I had a stick to steady myself," Jessie said, "I could hop on one leg."

Toady found a fat limb, bleached white and smooth. With it Jessie managed to hobble down the beach to the fire. But she knew she could never climb the dune.

She dropped to a log, keeping her left foot out straight, and wiggled out of her soaked jeans. A shower would feel so good.

"You need ice on that ankle," Allie said.

"Sure, Allie. Just run and get some from the refrigerator."

But Allie was already heading for the dune. Soon she returned waving a pajama-leg towel. "Here's dry clothes, too," she said, handing Jessie her shorts and top.

She ran to the water's edge and dipped the towel in a tide pool, then wrung it out and wrapped it around Jessie's ankle.

The cool cloth soothed the throbbing pain.

"I'll change it every little bit," Allie promised.

Allie scurried about, piling wood on the fire, making sure there was water on the clams, and sent Toady to fish.

Once, she disappeared up the hill and returned carrying their sleeping bags and Jessie's book. She draped one of the bags over a bleached chunk of driftwood and made a cozy chair for Jessie, then handed her the book.

"You just sit and read," Allie ordered, standing straight and placing her hands on her hips the way Mom often did.

Jessie couldn't keep her mind on the book for watching an Allie she'd never seen before. A take-charge Allie.

Had her sister really changed just this morning? Or had she been changing without anyone noticing? Even her color was different, a kind of shining brown now instead of the ashy shade it'd been before. And she had color in her cheeks. And Toady looked taller. Maybe because he'd lost some of his chubbiness. They'd all gotten thinner—and tanned. She thought about all the wood Toady had gathered. Both her sister and her brother were taking on responsibilities.

She laid her head back and let the sun warm her face and arms and legs. She remembered the day Allie had found the shovel and how excited she'd been. And the day she'd spotted the smoke beyond the rocks. It was Allie who shelled the chinquapin nuts. And Jessie remembered her saying that at least she could do two things well.

Do people change and you don't even notice? Maybe we're all changing, she thought. She glanced at Toady bent over his fishing line, frowning as he worked at fastening a hook. Where was his Adventure Man hat? He hadn't worn it since . . . maybe since he found the fishing line? Or even before.

Later, Toady returned, grinning as he held out three good-sized fish. Allie took them and got the knife. But when she stood looking at the fish, Jessie knew she couldn't bring herself to clean them.

"You want me to do that?" Jessie asked.

"I can," Toady said importantly, as he took the fish from Allie and found a flat rock. When he came back she was ready to heap seaweed on the coals.

"Careful," Jessie told her, "or the wet seaweed will steam and burn you bad."

Allie dropped the wet mass and jumped away as it sizzled and sputtered, spewing steam into the air. It still hissed as she gingerly placed the fish on top and covered them with a broad kelp leaf.

A few minutes later she took two long sticks and lifted the first fish onto a driftwood board to cool. Grinning, she reached for the next one. But as she did so, one of the sticks slipped and the fish dropped into the fire.

"No! Oh, no, no!" she screamed, jabbing at the fire with the sticks.

Jessie hobbled to the fire, where she took one of the sticks and dragged the charred mess into the sand.

"I tried to lift it and the sticks slipped, and it just fell," Allie cried through tears. "I'm sorry, Jessie, I'm sorry! I'll go without any. I just can't do anything right!"

"Allie, calm down," Jessie ordered, placing her arms around her sister. "You did great. Things like that just happen."

"But you wouldn't have dropped it," Allie wailed.

Jessie stifled a smile. "I might have. Now come on."

"We still have two fish," Toady told her. "And they're big ones."

"Hey, we better get the other one off the fire," Jessie said as she slid the sticks into the seaweed.

Allie joined them, still sniffling but eating her share.

"Allie," Jessie said, "I watched you this afternoon, doing stuff, taking care of me, and everything. I was really proud of you."

"Me, too," Toady declared.

Allie remained silent, but she gave them a smile.

After they'd eaten, Toady raced along the beach, dragging long whips of kelp, swinging them over his head, pretending some noisy game.

Allie came and sat in the sand beside Jessie. "Jessie," she said.

Jessie pulled her sister to her in a rush of love.

Allie rested her chin on her brown knees and brushed sand off her feet.

"Do you think we have a grandma?" she asked. Her dark eyes entreated Jessie. "Maybe?" She added in a small voice, "Somewhere?"

Jessie didn't answer at once, and Allie went on, "Melissa, you know?"

Jessie nodded. Melissa was Allie's friend at school.

"Well, she lives with her grandma, and she says nobody has anything to say about her except her grandma. No one at all, she says."

"I see. So if we had a grandma you think she might. . ."

"Don't you? Melissa says her grandma is the nicest person in the whole world." Allie sat quiet for several moments, then looked imploringly at Jessie. "Do you think if we had a grandma she'd take care of us and we wouldn't have to go back to Sherrill? Or maybe she'd say we could live with Mom and Pop?"

"Allie, I'll have to think about that. Okay?"

"Sure." With that she jumped up and poked more wood on the fire.

Jessie watched her sister. Didn't she realize they all had different fathers and how hard it would be to find any of them, let alone grandparents? They'd never talked about family or relatives because there weren't any, at least as far as Jessie knew. What did Allie's question mean? Was that her solution to their problem?

Chapter Twenty-Three

They all slept on the beach that night. By the next morning most of the swelling was gone, but Jessie's ankle pained her when she tried to put weight on it. She hobbled around the beach but dared not go into the rocky areas to gather clams.

When Allie insisted on digging clams, Jessie made her promise not to go far out. "Stay close to shore or I'll come after you."

"With that ankle?"

"With that ankle." She wrinkled her nose at her sister. After more than an hour Allie came back, complaining, "I only found four clams."

"The tide wasn't very low today," Jessie said, "and you had nothing to dig with."

"I'll catch lots of fish," Toady boasted, "so it won't matter. Maybe I'll catch a salmon."

Jessie stifled a chuckle. He really expects to catch a salmon, she thought. Well, maybe it's good to think big. She sighed, wondering if she thought big enough.

Allie disappeared up the hill, leaving Jessie alone. She hobbled out to the ocean side of the rocks and sat watching Toady fish.

The sun glinting off the water made her feel lazy, and she pondered Allie's question about a grandma. Maybe that's thinking big, too. Maybe it's possible, and I just can't see it. She lay back, letting the sun warm her, and closed her eyes. What if she found her father? If he had a mother, that would be her grandmother. Maybe she'd have red hair. Maybe there would be uncles, maybe an aunt. And if those people had children, they'd be her cousins. And when she found them they'd all be so glad because she'd been lost all this time.

Her eyes flew open. Stupid! Daydreaming about things that didn't exist. Or if they did she'd never know it. Why'd Sherrill have to make such a mess of things!

Toady caught only three perch, though he sat on the rock for hours. Allie came back with a container of berries. "Here's dessert," she said, grinning.

Jessie cooked the fish and clams after Allie found seaweed to steam them.

"I think we're getting used to eating only one meal. I haven't even been hungry all day," Jessie said.

"Me, either," Toady agreed, stuffing a big bite of fish into his mouth. "I sure am now, though. But not for clams!"

The late-day sky turned red and orange and cast a pink glow over the hills and on the water. But when the sun set it looked as though it had been cut in half. The top glowed red; then thick, gray fog obscured the center, and below hung the base of the round red ball. They watched as it slowly sank into a band of gray.

"That fog bank could come in tonight," Jessie said. "I think I can climb the dune now." But only a few steps in the loose sand sent pains shooting through her leg.

"You don't have to stay here just because I can't make it," she told the others.

Allie shook her head. "We'll stay together. Now I'm going up and pick some nuts for tomorrow. Want to help, Toady?"

"I can do them if you bring them down," Jessie called after them.

A few minutes later she heard loud shouts and jumped up.

"Get out! Go away! Get, get, get," Allie cried.

Jessie hobbled across the sand, fear clutching at her.

Toady yelled and made threatening noises.

"Allie, what's wrong?" she called, but the only answer was more shouting.

Her heart pounding, Jessie tried to climb the dune, but her ankle was too painful. At last she got down and crawled, urgency pulling her upward in spite of the agony, but she could move only a few feet at a time. The yelling above grew more insistent.

"Allie!" she cried, "What's happening?"

Toady appeared at the top of the dune. "Squirrels are gettin' our nuts. We're tryin' to chase them away."

Jessie collapsed on the sand, relief leaving her weak, laughing so hard she couldn't move. *Only squirrels.*

By the time Toady and Allie came back down, the sun had set and darkness was closing about them. Jessie still sat on the dune where she'd crawled.

"They got all the nuts," Toady announced.

"We couldn't scare them off, no matter what." Allie sat down and folded her arms across her chest. "Not fair. Why'd they have to take all our nuts."

"Allie, they have to eat, too," Jessie said. "Maybe they thought we were taking their nuts."

"They didn't have to be pigs! They could have left some!"

Jessie struggled to her feet, and at once Allie took her arm. "You need help?" she asked.

"No, I can walk." She stepped lightly on the sore foot and found that while it still hurt, the pain didn't shoot all through her leg as before. "I think it's better."

The fog rolled in that night and left everything sopping wet. They built up the fire and spent most of the next day drying sleeping bags, hanging them on a make-shift rack built of driftwood. By favoring her ankle, Jessie found she could walk on it.

That evening they banked the fire to burn all night. Toady and Allie carried their belongings back to the tree while Jessie made her way slowly up the dune.

After they were in their sleeping-bag bed beneath the tree, Allie said, "It feels like home, doesn't it, Jessie?"

Chapter Twenty-Four

"*It feels like home.*"

That's the first thing Jessie thought of the next morning. The surf's soft *shuuuushing* lulled her, and she opened her eyes to the criss-crossed green-gold branches above and remembered what Toady had said: "It's like the tree's hugging me."

"But it's *not* home," she told herself, jerking fully awake. She flung on her jacket and went slowly down the dune, still favoring her ankle. Soon she had the fire blazing. She fitted herself into a chunk of driftwood, grayed and smoothed by weather. Peaceful. Here she could think.

Home. The word had nagged at her mind for days. Not just a place to stay or be taken care of—the other foster homes had been that. Mom and Pop's was home because there was love. The thought seemed simple, so why hadn't she figured it out before?

But is it home if we can't live there? Now, while we're hiding? Even if we have to go back to Sherrill? Or get separated, sent to different foster homes? Jessie's insides felt shaky at the thought.

A seagull landed in the sand and strutted toward her, hoping she'd toss him some food, no doubt.

"Nothing for you," she said. "Nothing for any of

us." He raised white wings and flew, soaring to the ocean side of the sea stacks.

She closed her eyes. We can't go to a city. We can't go anywhere! She didn't even know what day it was. It seemed ages since she'd marked the tide book, and now the days all ran together. Thoughts tumbled about until her head felt as if it were stuffed with sand.

"We have to do *something*!" she said aloud, urgently. There's nothing to eat.

We're all so sick of clams—just the thought of them made her stomach turn—and Toady couldn't catch enough fish to keep them going. Dampness had ruined the blackberries, clotting them with white mildew. Only a niggling few dried-up salal berries still clung to the bushes. The nuts were gone.

The sun had tried to peek through, but now as she looked to the west, burgeoning gray clouds hung close to the horizon. She could hardly tell where the ocean ended and the sky began. Would it rain? A band of apprehension squeezed her chest. How could they keep dry?

She was so deep in her own thoughts that she jumped when Toady asked behind her, "Jessie, can we eat something?"

She looked at him and tried to smile, but her face felt stretched out of shape. "Wait a while," she said, trying to sound natural. Wait for what? Something to fall from the sky?

He looked at her for a moment, then turned and climbed back up the dune.

When she returned to the tree later, Allie had rolled the sleeping bags and piled them against the tree. She smoothed their sandy floor with a broom made from a tree branch.

"Where's Toady?" Jessie asked.

Allie shrugged and set her broom behind the tree. "I dunno. He came in and then went out the back door."

"Maybe he went to the faucet," Jessie decided. He still believed he'd find another chest of food.

Jasper. How long has it been since he said he'd be back? Well, it doesn't matter. We can't depend on other people. Just ourselves!

She walked out to the field and looked at all the plants growing there. If Pop were here he'd know which ones were okay to eat. He'd planned to teach them that, how to survive in the wild. The only wild plants she knew they could eat were dandelions, and she saw few of them here. The bright yellow flowers showed where they grew.

She picked one of the long, notched leaves and chewed on it, then made a face. Bitter. Mom sometimes gathered dandelion leaves and put them in salad, but they hadn't tasted like this. Maybe they were only good in spring. Or maybe this was a different kind and it was poisonous.

Jessie went beneath the tree and paced back and forth, peering at her watch every little bit. "Where has he gone?" she said at last. "Come on, Allie, we've got to find Toady."

They walked up to the faucet, then on to the house. Jessie felt strange as they climbed the steps to a porch. The front door was wide and carved, and it had a fancy metal handle instead of just a knob. They peered through a window.

"Jessie, what if there's food in the house?" Allie asked.

"We can't bother the house. We promised." Still, what if she tried a door and it opened? Would she go in? Take things? Would it be stealing? If they could pay for it later? Would that woman want them to starve?

Just then a shout came from up the hill. Toady ran toward them, shirtless and hugging a bundle close to his chest. He stopped and dropped his shirt, sending round, yellow apples rolling across the wooden floor.

Grinning, he said, "Look what I found."

Allie picked one up and breathed deeply. "They smell so good," she said as she gathered them.

"Where, Toady? Where'd you find them?" Jessie demanded.

It took a moment before he answered. "Across the fence and down a ways."

"You climbed that high fence?" Jessie cried.

Toady nodded. "There was a tree down there," he pointed, "and I shinnied up and over the fence." He grinned at his feat, then handed her a newspaper. "Look, we're in it."

He spread it open before them, showing three photos, their last year's school pictures. The headline read, MISSING CHILDREN FEARED DROWNED. But below their pictures was another. Of a woman. Crying. Sherrill.

"What's she doing there?" Allie cried around a mouthful of apple.

"Who is she?" Toady asked.

"It's Sherrill," Allie said.

Toady just said, "Oh."

Jessie read aloud, "Authorities said today the missing Cloud children may have tried to hide in caves south of the Harmon farm and were caught by high tides. A sleeping bag found near the caves has been identified by the Harmons. Sherrill Cloud, mother of the missing children, is staying in Mills Beach while the search continues. In tears, she told authorities she loved her children and begged anyone who might know their whereabouts to come forward. The children were removed from her home and placed in foster care three years ago. For the past two years they have lived with the Harmon family in this community."

When she'd finished reading, Jessie laid the paper on the porch and looked at Toady.

"How did you get the apples, Toady?"

"I told you," he said, his mouth almost too full to speak. "I climbed the tree and dropped over the fence. Then I walked down the road, and I saw a whole limb hanging outside the fence. Covered with apples. There weren't any houses where I could see them, so I climbed up the bank and picked them. There's lots more, too."

"Where was the paper?"

"In a paper box." He said it slowly, looking down at his feet.

"Toady! What if someone saw you? What will the people do when they find their paper missing?"

Toady shrugged one shoulder. "Probably call the newspaper office and complain like Pop does sometimes."

Laughter and scolding were all mixed up in Jessie's thoughts. Toady was probably right. Still, she couldn't have him climbing over fences, helping himself to whatever he found.

"The apples taste awful good," Allie put in, as though to defend Toady.

Jessie sighed. She picked up an apple and closed her eyes, savoring the sweet aromatic smell, as she bit into the juicy fruit. She wrapped the rest of the apples in Toady's shirt and started down the hill toward the tree. At least they would eat, and if they could find a few clams or mussels maybe they could stand to eat them along with the fruit.

Once back beneath the tree, Jessie told Toady. "It's good we have the apples, and I'm glad to read the paper and find out what's happening. But Toady, promise me you won't do that again."

He looked at her for a long time, his blue eyes serious. "I guess," he mumbled.

They each ate two apples, and Jessie put the others away.

"I'm going fishin'," Toady announced. "We can't just eat apples."

Jessie stared after him. How grown up he sounded. Taking responsibility for all of them.

The girls followed Toady to the beach. The tide was full high, so there was no chance of finding either clams or mussels. Jessie looked out over the ocean. To the west, clouds the color of the sea rocks had moved up the sky. The air smelled watery. *It can't rain.*

Toady caught only two fish, and Jessie cleaned and cooked them.

By late afternoon the sky had turned so dark it seemed like nighttime, and the wind blew sand along the beach. The sea looked rumpled and angry, and waves thundered against the cliffs.

As they started back up the dune, three huge raindrops splattered on Jessie's arm. Black clouds hung straight overhead. Big drops fell all around them, and the ground smelled of summer dust, newly wet.

Chapter Twenty-Five

"*H*urry," Jessie told Allie and Toady as they climbed the dune. Beneath the tree she scurried about, gathering up the thin plastic tarps they used under their sleeping bags.

"What're you doing?" Allie asked.

"Making a tent," she said as she draped the tarps over a limb. "We have to keep stuff dry." She tore strips from one of their pajama-leg towels, spread the tarps, and tied the corners to low branches.

She took two black garbage bags from her pack and laid them on the ground beneath the tent, then spread the sleeping bags on top.

"It stopped," Toady said, holding up a branch. "Hey, Jessie, it's not raining."

Jessie blew out a long breath and stood up.

"See," Toady cried, holding the branch above his head.

Jessie went outside. The rain had stopped. But low against the ocean lay long gray furrows of cloud.

They each ate two more apples. The air grew cold, and they put on their jackets. Jessie kept an eye on the clouds.

Somberly, Allie asked, "Where'll we sleep, Jessie?"

"On the sleeping bags," she answered, "but we'll have to sit up or the tarps won't cover us. We need to get in place before it gets so dark we can't see." She found three remaining trash bags and poked holes in the bottom of each.

"Here," she said, "pull these over your head."

"What for?" Toady demanded.

"Go ahead. It'll keep you dry."

He put on the bag and laughed. "I'm wearing a dress," he said. He wiggled his hips, and the girls laughed.

"Now, we'll sit under the tent and wrap the sleeping bags around us."

As daylight faded into blackness, the rain began in earnest, not just big plopping drops, but a slow drizzle that made the air feel heavy and promised to soak everything.

"We have to crowd together," Jessie told them.

"I'm here, Toady," Allie said. "Scoot over next to me."

"Let me have some room," Jessie said, cuddling beside Allie and pulling the bags around them.

"It feels like a cocoon," Allie said. "How long will we stay here?"

"Until the rain stops. Now sit still, and if you change position tell me first, okay?"

At first she thought the tree might turn the rain away. But after a while drops of water plunked on the plastic draped above their heads.

Jessie's feet stuck out and were soon soaked. She tried to tuck them under, but she was afraid that if she moved she might wreck their makeshift nest.

Both children slept, Allie draped across Jessie's lap and Toady snuggled next to her. Jessie's arms tingled and her legs felt stiff. Before long, water seeped in and she sat in a puddle.

She must have slept at last. Much later she opened her eyes to bright light.

Sunlight!

When Jessie moved, cold water trickled down their necks, making all three squeal.

"Crawl out easy," she said.

"Did the fire go out?" Allie asked.

"The fire!" Jessie cried.

She jumped up and ducked under wet branches, getting a cold shower. She hadn't thought of it, with trying to keep them all dry. Shivering, she plunged down the steep dune, wet sand clinging to her feet. "Don't let it be out," she prayed.

No smoke spiraled upward from the stump, which loomed out of the mist.

Jessie hesitated, afraid to look. She knelt and peered into the hole, a charred black opening.

"Dead out."

But when she reached into the hole she felt warmth. Heart pounding, she dug into her pockets for paper but found none. The driftwood was sopping wet. She'd have to go back to the tree and tear more pages from her book.

When she returned to the stump she ripped out several pages, wadded them and held them tight against the charred wood. Although she felt heat, nothing happened. When her arm seemed ready to fall off, she pulled the paper back. Two little scorched spots marred the page.

"Please, please," she prayed as she leaned down once more, poking the paper far back, again pressing it tightly against the wood. Heat warmed her hands, but that was all. Finally, she wadded several pages and stuffed them beneath the stump. Then she knelt and, taking a deep breath, blew as hard as she could. Again and again she blew.

Was that a wisp of smoke? She smelled smoldering paper. She blew and blew and blew. Suddenly a tiny flame flickered, then crept slowly, eating its way around the edges of the paper.

She wadded page after page and tossed each one into the flames until the charred stump began to glow red once more.

Her face spread into a grin. She felt like shouting with joy. But now she needed wood—dry wood.

Toady's wood had been piled so well that a few pieces at the bottom of the stack remained dry. She stuffed them over the flame, a few at a time.

Soon she had a blazing fire once more. She piled on more and more wood, then stood before the opening, soaking up the warmth.

She hadn't even realized Toady and Allie had come down to the beach until they moved closer to dry out.

The sun was almost as warm, shining down, making the air clammy. They'd have to spread everything to dry soon.

Her book lay in the sand, the cover bent open and showing the ragged edges where she'd ripped out pages. Like a dead bird. Why hadn't she thought to use the newspaper Toady had brought? Because she was too frantic, she guessed.

Allie held an apple for each of them, and they sat on a log and ate. Soon Toady jumped up and raced down the beach. Jessie watched as he hung headfirst over a log, hunting firewood.

"Jessie, how come Sherrill's here?" Allie asked.

Jessie had read in the newspaper how Sherrill blamed Mom and Pop, and that she was the one who insisted a guard be posted at the Harmon's, but she hadn't told Allie and Toady that. They seldom read a newspaper themselves.

It also quoted a Children's Services spokesman as saying, "When they are found, they will be returned to Multnomah County where we can see to their safety." She hadn't told them that either.

"I'm not sure." After a moment Jessie asked, "Allie, do you think Sherrill wants to be different?"

Allie looked up quickly, then down at the ground. "No."

"But what if she does?"

"She don't." Allie squatted in the sand, her toes digging in. She piled sand over her feet.

"We don't know that for sure."

"I do." Allie still looked away, not meeting Jessie's eyes.

She couldn't tell Allie about the other day. The day

she slashed the stick across the tide pool and scared all the little crabs. But it hung in her mind like a shadow, a shadow she couldn't see behind.

"Wonder what happened to her to make her that way? Wonder why she started drinking and—stuff?"

For a long time Allie sat making marks in the sand with her fingers. At last she looked at Jessie and declared, "She's probably always been bad. I just think some people are. *Bad*."

As though finished with their conversation, Allie got up and poked more wood on the fire.

Jessie sat thinking. Was Allie right? I don't want to live with her, she decided, but I don't hate her anymore.

Chapter Twenty-Six

*H*ot, gritty sand hugged Jessie's bare feet as she lazed along the beach. The ocean's soft rumble and the humid air soothed her spirit. She dropped into the sand and lounged against a driftwood log. Peaceful. Except . . .

Except they had no food.

The apples were gone. Toady had caught no fish for days, and high tides during the day kept them from gathering clams or mussels. At Toady's insistence Jessie finally let him go back to the apple tree. She and Allie climbed the hill and waited anxiously beside the fence until he returned.

But he carried only seven apples. "Somebody picked the rest," he said glumly.

"Never mind, Toady," Jessie told him. "We'll each eat one now and another before we go to sleep tonight. We can share the last one tomorrow. We'll drink lots of water so we'll feel full."

She cut three apples into quarters, and they ate them, then nibbled every bit from the core except the seeds.

What have we gained? she asked herself. The answer came at once: We've changed. We're different than we were. She felt stronger, less afraid of what might happen to them. "It's like everything has changed," she said aloud, "only nothing's changed. Except us."

She glanced toward the rock where Toady sat, his fishing line dangling in the surf.

Allie's question about a grandmother kept flitting into her thoughts. Was that Allie's solution to their problems? An impossible fantasy. Did Allie really believe it was possible?

Then another thought rushed in. That's what my daydreaming about a father is! A fantasy. Trying to draw hope from some shadowy memory—a memory that probably isn't even real. Silly notions we concocted and wanted to believe. Like people thinking they'll win the lottery! "We have to get real!" she said aloud. "Nobody is going to rescue us. We have to do it ourselves."

She got up and strode through the baking-hot sand.

They had to go back, she knew that. But it didn't feel like failure. She remembered how beaten down she'd felt when the raccoons stole their food. But they hadn't stayed down. What counts is when we're grown up. Just knowing nothing's forever, we can deal with it.

Thinking about how they'd taken care of each other, managed even when things went wrong, made Jessie feel proud in a way she never had before.

We've found ways to survive, but it's more than that. Maybe it's what happens inside a person that counts the most. Everybody taking responsibility. Allie giving up her fears. Her own changed feelings toward Sherrill.

She sat down on a whitened stump and ran her fingers along the patterns and designs that had formed as its surface had bleached. Like a beautiful etching, only done by sun and weather. Scrolls and tracings sketched in shades of black and brown and gray against the soft white, creating something beautiful. Happening slowly over years while the stump lay here, half buried in sand, not knowing it was changing.

"There's no fish in there," Toady called, as he trudged up to her, shattering her reverie.

Jessie smiled at her brother, noticing how much browner he'd become. "It doesn't matter, Toady," she told him. "We'll manage."

After Toady and Allie fell asleep, Jessie wandered out to the dune, then halfway down, where she sat watching the stars slowly appear. The evening star burned the brightest, but gradually cold lights peppered the whole sky.

Jasper's words sang in her head. Words like *goals* and *take charge of your life* and, most of all, beacon. Beacons guided you, kept you safe.

The sand grated her elbows and she brushed it off.

"Dad is my beacon," Jasper had said.

Are Mom and Pop our beacon?

As if the stars had sung it to her, she knew—and knowing sent a shiver through her—home isn't a place. It's people. People who love you. People who will always be there, helping you get through whatever happens.

Pop's words that last night rang in her head. "'This

is your home. Forever. No matter what happens.'"

No matter what happens. Pop was telling them something. That they'd always have a home no matter where they lived. Like Jasper saying he lived in two places, two worlds.

Even if we have to go back to Portland, and she guessed they probably would, Mom and Pop would still be there for them, keeping in touch, keeping track of them. As long as Mom and Pop knew where they were, they couldn't get lost from one another. Even if they had to go to different foster homes.

We can be in charge of our lives! Nothing will ever be the same again. We never before lived where the caring went on and on. And in a few years I'll be grown up and can take care of Allie and Toady.

She lay back in the sand and gazed upward. The sky was a black bowl with specks of light gleaming through pinholes.

Take charge—take charge. Excitement built inside her, made her feel light as air, as if she could float out over the sea, up among the stars. She half-closed her eyes, and the stars came close enough to touch. She floated with them.

Music seemed to sing in her head, or was it coming from the stars? And with the music a power stirred through her. An idea was forming in her mind, like a wave swelling, growing, curling, until its power carved troughs in solid stone. Power made things happen.

Because somebody cares, we have a power we never had before.

Her eyes flew wide open and she sat straight up. The stars faded back into place.

Ideas were jamming her mind. *We can be in charge in some ways. We can make some decisions.*

Paddling her legs, she began to slip downward in the loose sand, still warm from the sun. She felt a grin stretching her face. Faster, faster, she went, shoving sand to the sides, flying down the dune. Free, free!

"I can do it!" she cried when she reached the beach, elated from gliding over the sand, and from something more.

She raced to the edge of the waves. Cold foam rippled over her ankles—to her knees—then drew back, pulling sand from beneath her feet. She waited for the next wave, looking across the dark ocean.

Were the hermit crabs out there? Still scurrying about on the bottom of the sea? In someothers' shells, but in charge of their lives.

"Like us." She spoke the words softly, reverently, like a promise.

Chapter Twenty-Seven

$\mathcal{T}$he gray sky above the tree lightened, until Jessie could make out the shapes of leaves. She got up and went outside. The ocean's roar and the deep rumble of gravel being pulled by the tide were the only sounds. When she reached the point where she could see the ledge, waves spewed over it.

If only she knew which day it was. How long had they been here? Nine days? Ten? It could be August 22nd or 23rd. But it could be only the 21st, too. And according to her tide book the first chance to cross would be on the 25th. It might be two or even three days before the morning low would come late enough to let them cross in daylight. Two or three days with nothing to eat. Still, they wouldn't starve.

Hunger was funny. Most of the time she felt no different from when they'd eaten. Then, unexpectedly, a pang would remind her. Like her stomach saying, "Hey, I'm empty." Grinning, she patted her belly. "Just have to wait," she said. They wouldn't starve.

Neither of the kids had complained. With a sigh she went back to the tree, where Toady and Allie were putting on their shoes.

"Come out to our patio," she told them. "I have something to tell you." They came and sat in the sand. Looking at their sober faces, some of her excitement from last night seeped away. What if she was wrong? No, there was no other choice.

"We have to go back," she began, feeling at a loss to communicate her feelings.

"I know," Allie said, as she sifted sand through her fingers. "I figured that out when it rained."

"You okay with that?"

Allie met Jessie's eyes. "Yes."

"See, I figure, it's . . . "

"Jessie, I'm not scared of stuff anymore. And I can stand up for myself. It's probably going to be the pits sometimes, but we'll make it."

Jessie smiled. "We are different, stronger. But it's more than that."

She explained, stumbling over her words, hoping she was making sense.

Allie sat making scroll marks in the sand the whole time Jessie spoke.

"Will Sherrill get us?" Toady asked, a scared look on his face.

"No!" Allie declared. "We won't live with her. Ever." Then she looked at Jessie. "When will we leave?" she asked.

That was the hard part.

"If I figured right, we can't cross the ledge for two, maybe even three days. Not when it's daylight, and we won't do it in the dark again."

"No way," Allie said.

Toady sat watching them.

"But," Allie said as she dug her feet into the sand,

"we got along here, we can do anything."

Jessie grinned, and Allie's brown eyes met her own. She understands, Jessie decided.

"I'm going to get some water," Toady said.

When he'd disappeared, Allie smiled. "He still hopes he'll find another ice chest full of food," she said.

It was true. Toady's morning ritual was going for water, but both girls knew his real reason.

Moments later they heard Toady's urgent yelling. The girls jumped to their feet and ran.

"Did he find it, you think?" Allie wondered aloud as they darted up the hill.

They stopped at the last salal patch. There, grinning beside Toady, stood Jasper, holding a brown grocery sack in both hands.

"It's Jasper!" Toady yelled. "An' guess what he's got?"

"Hi," the boy said. "I thought maybe you could use this." He held out the large paper bag.

Jessie took it and savored the salty smell of ham.

Even before they reached the tree, Toady was clutching at the bag. "Boy, are we hungry!" he cried.

Her hands shaking, Jessie slid out a tray heaped with warm biscuits, ham, and slices of orange.

Toady and Allie dove in at once, picking up ham in one hand and a biscuit, swimming with butter, in the other. Jessie's stomach felt as though it were grasping for the delicious odors.

"Thank you," Jessie said, trying not to seem as greedy as the kids.

"Look," Jasper said, "I never dreamed you'd still be out here like this. My dad called the same day I was here. He did get to come to the states—to Los Angeles—for a week, and he had me fly down to be with him." He looked at his feet. "We had to leave at four the next morning, so I didn't have a chance to tell you.

"Mom and Fred picked me up at the airport last night. I couldn't believe it when they said you were still missing. I—I wondered if you were okay."

Jessie heaved a sigh.

"But, golly, I should have told Fred. He could have helped you. Look," he said, "you got—" he hesitated "—anything else to eat?"

Before Jessie could speak, Toady shouted, "No!"

"We *had* food—" Jessie began.

"—but the raccoons got it!" Toady finished.

"Then we just had fish and clams," Allie put in.

"An' berries. An' nuts till the squirrels got them all," Toady added.

Jasper glanced around their tree camp. "I see you found the ice chest. I hoped that would help."

"It did," Jessie said as she bit into a biscuit.

"I knew you left that chest," Toady cried, his mouth stuffed full. "We can stay here forever now we've got something to eat!" he exclaimed.

"Toady!" Jessie cried, feeling her face go hot.

Jasper grinned. "Never mind," he said softly.

"We're going to the beach," Allie said. They had new energy now that they'd eaten.

Jasper watched as Toady and Allie ran to the dune

and slid down. He looked at Jessie thoughtfully. "Hey, I'm sorry. I should have brought stuff that'd last. Cans or something. I just wasn't thinking."

Suddenly Jessie felt close to tears at his apology. She took her food and went out to the sand. Jasper followed.

"The kids call this our patio," she said.

"I can see why." He looked at her. "I can't believe you've managed out here all this time. You know, you're one gutsy gal."

Jessie flushed.

"So, what happens now?"

Jessie hesitated. How could she make him understand? "You helped, you know?"

"How?"

"By the things you told me."

She explained, hesitating, hoping he understood how they had changed, how that had made everything else change.

Jessie concentrated on eating, avoiding Jasper's eyes. When she looked up he was watching her.

"You probably made the best decision," he said.

She nodded, suddenly feeling sad that their adventure was ending. She glanced up to her reading perch.

"When will you leave? Mom will let me use the car if . . ."

"No," she said quickly. "We'll go back the same way we came. Only I don't know when the tide's low enough to cross the ledge."

"You don't have a tide book?"

"We do. But we lost track of the days."

"It's August twenty-fourth."

She felt her face spread into a grin. "The twenty-fourth? We can cross tomorrow morning!" She dug her tide book from her pocket just to be sure. Reading, she said, "Tide's low at four-forty-eight in the morning. Not a minus, but low enough, I think. We can cross as soon as it's daylight."

Jasper stood up. "Look, can I come back and go with you? I want to see this cave or tunnel or whatever it is. Besides, I'll bring breakfast, so you can eat first. Actually, I'll be back tonight with supper."

Jessie laughed at the way he stumbled over his words.

After Jasper left, they spent the rest of the day packing everything into their backpacks, cleaning up around the tree, and making sure the fire under the stump was dead out. Toady sat on his fishing rock. Jessie knew he would miss it, but she told herself this would always be a special time—a special place in their memories.

That evening Jasper returned carrying two boxes. The pungent odor of onions mingled with meat and relish told Jessie what was inside.

"What've you got?" Toady cried at once.

"Super burgers," Jasper announced as he opened the box and removed three meals covered with paper plates that had been decorated with lop-sided golden arches. "And french fries."

"McDonald's!" Toady cried.

"How'd you get them?" Allie asked. "We don't have McDonald's here."

Jessie met Jasper's amused glance.

"Actually, they're my own version," he said as Allie and Toady took theirs. "The McDonald's touch was Fred's idea. My stepfather."

"You told?" Jessie cried.

Jasper held the third plate out to her. "I had to. He caught me broiling the burgers and asked a bunch of questions. But he won't tell."

"I guess it doesn't matter now anyhow," Jessie said.

"Can we eat on the beach?" Allie asked.

Jessie shrugged, and she and Jasper followed the younger children. They sat on logs while they ate.

When they'd finished, Toady and Allie ran in circles in the sand. Toady picked up a long whip of brown kelp and swung it close to the sand, whirling around and around. Allie jumped it on each turn. Faster and faster he spun until finally they both dropped in the sand.

"I'm dizzy," Toady said, clowning.

"Better get up and unwind in the other direction," Jasper told him, as he and Jessie laughed.

Allie came and sat nearby. "That was fun, but I'm wore out."

"You never missed once," Jessie told her.

"Yeah," Jasper added, "I couldn't do that."

Allie grinned. She got up and ran along the beach, stamping on the little seaweed bladders, popping them like tiny balloons.

Toady came and stood in front of Jasper. "What has eyes and can't hear?" he asked.

"Don't you mean *see*?"

"Oh, I made a dumb mistake," Toady crowed, mimicking Pop.

"An' what has ears and can't smell?"

Jasper grabbed him and swung him up into the air. "I think someone is trying to trip me up."

"No, no," Toady cried. "You didn't answer."

"Here's your answer," Jasper said as he deposited Toady on an outcropping of one of the sea stacks.

"Oh, I can get down," Toady said, doubling over in laughter. "Just watch." He crept along the rock and soon jumped back onto the sand.

Jasper came back and sat down beside Jessie. "I need to get back to the house. But, look, I wrote my phone number in this address book," he said. "If you ever need anything, call me. I know you can call the Harmons, but—well, I'd like you to have my number, too. You might just call to let me know how things are going. Or write. My address is there, too."

A lump came to her throat as his gray eyes smiled down at her. Somebody else who cares about us.

"Sure," she said, hardly able to speak. "We'll keep in touch."

Chapter Twenty-Eight

They were up and had the sleeping bags rolled by the time Jasper arrived the following morning. He set a light down in the semidarkness.

"Here's a trash bag if you need it," he said. "I'll pick this stuff up on my way back."

He opened a box and handed them each a bun with sausage and eggs stuffed inside. "I thought these would be fast, so we can get started."

They ate in silence, then wadded the papers and put them in the trash. Finally there was nothing more to do. And it was time. Light enough to see.

Jessie looked at each of them, then picked up her backpack and moved into the morning mist. Soon the sun would be out, hot. By that time they would be home.

When she reached the place where they could see the ledge, water churned several inches below it.

"So this is it?" Jasper asked as he helped Toady climb up. "The famous ledge. Golly, all the time I've lived here, I never knew it was there."

Allie and Toady moved across cautiously while Jasper carried their things.

"You crossed this in the dark!" Jasper exclaimed. "Wow!"

The others moved on, their voices muffled in the cave, then fading until Jessie couldn't hear them at all.

The ocean rumbled, and waves slapped the rock below Jessie's feet. She stood on the narrow shelf, looking back at her tree. A lump filled her throat so that she couldn't swallow. She closed her eyes, wanting that goldy-green image to stay in her mind forever.

"I'll be back someday," she promised, more to herself than to the tree. "Even if it's not till I'm grown up."

Finally she turned and crossed the ledge to the cave. As she entered the dim interior, waves echoed off the wet walls and gravel crunched beneath her feet. Ahead a circle of light gleamed, like a beacon.